CHEAP STEEL SPOONS

The big man with no shirt came back across the room with five cheap steel spoons. The girl with the green hair giggled. "I ain't never ate no live brain before."

"It's stuzzy stuff, Rainbow," Phil told her. "This oughta be a good brain. Full of chemicals, I imagine."

Haf-N-Haf seemed to be having trouble starting the little cutting machine. It was a variable heat-blade. They were going to cut off the top of Sta-Hi's skull and eat his brain with those cheap steel spoons. He would be able to watch them . . . at first.

Someone started screaming.

Other Avon Books by
Rudy Rucker

Coming Soon

WETWARE

Software

Rudy Rucker

AVON
PUBLISHERS OF BARD, CAMELOT, DISCUS AND FLARE BOOKS

An excerpt from this book appeared in *The Mind's I*, copyright © 1981 by Douglas R. Hofstadter and Daniel C. Dennett. Published by Basic Books.

AVON BOOKS
A division of
The Hearst Corporation
105 Madison Avenue
New York, New York 10016

Copyright © 1982 by Rudy Rucker
Front cover illustration by Joe Devito
Published by arrangement with the author
ISBN: 0-380-70177-4

First Avon Printing: October 1987

AVON TRADEMARK REG. U.S. PAT. OFF. AND IN OTHER COUNTRIES, MARCA REGISTRADA, HECHO EN U.S.A.

Printed in the U.S.A.

K-R 10 9 8 7 6 5 4 3 2 1

For Al Humboldt, Embry Rucker,
and Dennis Poague.

Chapter One

Cobb Anderson would have held out longer, but you don't see dolphins every day. There were twenty of them, fifty, rolling in the little gray waves, wicketting up out of the water. It was good to see them. Cobb took it for a sign and went out for his evening sherry an hour early.

The screen door slapped shut behind him and he stood uncertainly for a moment, dazed by the late afternoon sun. Annie Cushing watched him from her window in the cottage next door. Beatles music drifted out past her.

"You forgot your hat," she advised. He was still a good-looking man, barrel-chested and bearded like Santa Claus. She wouldn't have minded getting it on with him, if he weren't so . . .

"Look at the dolphins, Annie. I don't need a hat. Look how happy they are. I don't need a hat and I don't need a wife." He started toward the asphalt road, walking stiffly across the crushed white shells.

Annie went back to brushing her hair. She wore it white and long, and she kept it thick with hormone spray. She was sixty and not too brittle to hug. She wondered idly if Cobb would take her to the Golden Prom next Friday.

The long last chord of "Day in the Life" hung in the air. Annie couldn't have said which song she had just heard—after fifty years her responses to the music were all but extinguished—but she walked across the room to turn the stack of records over. *If only something would happen*, she thought for the thousandth time. *I get so tired of being me.*

At the Superette, Cobb selected a chilled quart of cheap sherry and a damp paper bag of boiled peanuts. And he wanted something to look at.

The Superette magazine selection was nothing compared to what you could get over in Cocoa. Cobb settled finally for a love-ad newspaper called *Kiss and Tell*. It was always good and weird . . . most of the advertisers were seventy-year-old hippies like himself. He folded the first-page picture under so that only the headline showed. PLEASE PHEEZE ME.

Funny how long you can laugh at the same jokes, Cobb thought, waiting to pay. Sex seemed odder all the time. He noticed the man in front of him, wearing a light-blue hat blocked from plastic mesh.

If Cobb concentrated on the hat he saw an irregular blue cylinder. But if he let himself look through the holes in the mesh he could see the meek curve of the bald head underneath. Skinny neck and a light-bulb head, clawing in his change. A friend.

"Hey, Farker."

Farker finished rounding up his nickels, then turned his body around. He spotted the bottle.

"Happy Hour came early today." A note of remonstrance. Farker worried about Cobb.

"It's Friday. Pheeze me tight." Cobb handed Farker the paper.

"Seven eighty-five," the cashier said to Cobb. Her white hair was curled and hennaed. She had a deep tan. Her flesh had a pleasingly used and oily look to it.

Cobb was surprised. He'd already counted money into his hand. "I make it six fifty." Numbers began sliding around in his head.

"I meant my box number," the cashier said with a toss of her head. "In the *Kiss and Tell*." She smiled coyly and took Cobb's money. She was proud of her ad this month. She'd gone to a studio for the picture.

Farker handed the paper back to Cobb outside. "I can't look at this, Cobb. I'm still a happily married man, God help me."

"You want a peanut?"

"Thanks." Farker extracted a soggy shell from the lit
tle bag. There was no way his spotted and trembling old
hands could have peeled the nut, so he popped it whole
into his mouth. After a minute he spit the hull out.

They walked towards the beach, eating pasty peanuts.
They wore no shirts, only shorts and sandals. The after-
noon sun beat pleasantly on their backs. A silent Mr.
Frostee truck cruised past.

Cobb cracked the screw-top on his dark-brown bottle
and took a tentative first sip. He wished he could remember the box number the cashier had just told him.
Numbers wouldn't stay still for him anymore. It was hard
to believe he'd ever been a cybernetician. His memory
ranged back to his first robots and how they'd learned to
bop . . .

"Food drop's late again," Farker was saying. "And
I hear there's a new murder cult up in Daytona. They're
called the Little Kidders." He wondered if Cobb could
hear him. Cobb was just standing there with empty col-
orless eyes, a yellow stain of sherry on the dense white
hair around his lips.

"Food drop," Cobb said, suddenly coming back. He
had a way of re-entering a conversation by confidently
booming out the last phrase which had registered. "I've
still got a good supply."

"But be sure to eat some of the new food when it
comes," Farker cautioned. "For the vaccines. I'll tell
Annie to remind you."

"Why is everybody so interested in staying alive? I
left my wife and came down here to drink and die in
peace. *She* can't wait for me to kick off. So why . . ."
Cobb's voice caught. The fact of the matter was that he
was terrified of death. He took a quick, medicinal slug
of sherry.

"If you were peaceful, you wouldn't drink so much,"
Farker said mildly. "Drinking is the sign of an unresolved conflict."

"No *kidding*," Cobb said heavily. In the golden
warmth of the sun, the sherry had taken quick effect.
"Here's an unresolved conflict for you." He ran a fin-

gernail down the vertical white scar on his furry chest.
"I don't have the money for another second-hand heart.
In a year or two this cheapie's going to poop out on
me."

Farker grimaced. "So? *Use* your two years."

Cobb ran his finger back up the scar, as if zipping it
up. "I've seen what it's like, Farker. I've had a taste of
it. It's the worst thing there is." He shuddered at the
dark memory . . . teeth, ragged clouds . . . and fell silent.

Farker glanced at his watch. Time to get going or
Cynthia would . . .

"You know what Jimi Hendrix said?" Cobb asked.
Recalling the quote brought the old resonance back into
his voice. "When it's my time to die, I'm going to be
the one doing it. So as long as I'm alive, you let me live
my way."

Farker shook his head. "Face it, Cobb, if you drank
less you'd get a lot more out of life." He raised his hand
to cut off his friend's reply. "But I've got to get home.
Bye bye."

"Bye."

Cobb walked to the end of the asphalt and over a low
dune to the edge of the beach. No one was there today,
and he sat down under his favorite palm tree.

The breeze had picked up a little. Warmed by the
sand, it lapped at Cobb's face, buried under white whisk-
ers. The dolphins were gone.

He sipped sparingly at his sherry and let the memories
play. There were only two thoughts to be avoided: death
and his abandoned wife Verena. The sherry kept them
away.

The sun was going down behind him when he saw the
stranger. Barrel-chest, erect posture, strong arms and legs
covered with curly hair, a round white beard. Like Santa
Claus, or like Ernest Hemingway the year he shot himself.

"Hello, Cobb," the man said. He wore sungoggles
and looked amused. His shorts and sportshirt glittered.

"Care for a drink?" Cobb gestured at the half-empty
bottle. He wondered who, if anyone, he was talking to.

"No thanks," the stranger said, sitting down. "It doesn't do anything for me."

Cobb stared at the man. Something about him . . .

"You're wondering who I am," the stranger said, smiling. "I'm you."

"You who?"

"You me." The stranger used Cobb's own tight little smile on him. "I'm a mechanical copy of your body."

The face seemed right and there was even the scar from the heart transplant. The only difference between them was how alert and healthy the copy looked. Call him Cobb Anderson$_2$. Cobb$_2$ didn't drink. Cobb envied him. He hadn't had a completely sober day since he had the operation and left his wife.

"How did you get here?"

The robot waved a hand palm up. Cobb liked the way the gesture looked on someone else. "I can't tell you," the machine said. "You know how most people feel about us."

Cobb chuckled his agreement. He should know. At first the public had been delighted that Cobb's moon-robots had evolved into intelligent boppers. That had been before Ralph Numbers had led the 2001 revolt. After the revolt, Cobb had been tried for treason. He focussed back on the present.

"If you're a bopper, then how can you be . . . here?" Cobb waved his hand in a vague circle taking in the hot sand and the setting sun. "It's too hot. All the boppers I know of are based on supercooled circuits. Do you have a refrigeration unit hidden in your stomach?"

Anderson$_2$ made another familiar hand-gesture. "I'm not going to tell you yet, Cobb. Later you'll find out. Just take this . . . ." The robot fumbled in its pocket and brought out a wad of bills. "Twenty-five grand. We want you to get the flight to Disky tomorrow. Ralph Numbers will be your contact up there. He'll meet you at the Anderson room in the museum."

Cobb's heart leapt at the thought of seeing Ralph Numbers again. Ralph, his first and finest model, the one who had set all the others free. But . . .

"I can't get a visa," Cob said. "You know that. I'm not allowed to leave the Gimmie territory."

"Let *us* worry about that," the robot said urgently. "There'll be someone to help you through the formalities. We're working on it right now. And I'll stand in for you while you're gone. No one'll be the wiser."

The intensity of his double's tone made Cobb suspicious. He took a drink of sherry and tried to look shrewd. "What's the point of all this? Why should I want to go to the Moon in the first place? And why do the boppers want me there?"

Anderson$_2$ glanced around the empty beach and leaned close. "We want to make you immortal, Dr. Anderson. After all you did for us, it's the least we can do."

Immortal! The word was like a window flung open. With death so close nothing had mattered. But if there was a way out . . .

"How?" Cobb demanded. In his excitement he rose to his feet. "How will you do it? Will you make me young again, too?"

"Take it easy," the robot said, also rising. "Don't get over-excited. Just trust us. With our supplies of tank-grown organs we can rebuild you from the ground up. And you'll get as much interferon as you need."

The machine stared into Cobb's eyes, looking honest. Staring back, Cobb noticed that they hadn't gotten the irises quite right. The little ring of blue was too flat and even. The eyes were, after all, just glass, unreadable glass.

The double pressed the money into Cobb's hand. "Take the money and get the shuttle tomorrow. We'll arrange for a young man called Sta-Hi to help you at the spaceport."

Music was playing, wheedling closer. A Mr. Frostee truck, the same one Cobb had seen before. It was white, with a big freezer-box in back. There was a smiling giant plastic ice-cream cone mounted on top of the cab. Cobb's double gave him a pat on the shoulder and trotted up the beach.

When he reached the truck, the robot looked back and flashed a smile. Yellow teeth in the white beard. For the first time in years, Cobb loved himself, the erect strut, the frightened eyes. "Good-bye," he shouted, waving the money. "And thanks!"

Cobb Anderson$_2$ jumped into the soft-ice-cream truck next to the driver, a fat short-haired man with no shirt. And then the Mr. Frostee truck drove off, its music silenced again. It was dusk now. The sound of the truck's motor faded into the ocean's roar. If only it was true.

But it had to be! Cobb was holding twenty-five thousand-dollar bills. He counted them twice to make sure. And then he scrawled the figure $25000 in the sand and looked at it. That was a lot.

As the darkness fell he finished the sherry and, on a sudden impulse, put the money in the bottle and buried it next to his tree in a meter of sand. The excitement was wearing off now, and fear was setting in. Could the boppers *really* give him immortality with surgery and interferon?

It seemed unlikely. A trick. But why would the boppers lie to him? Surely they remembered all the good things he'd done for them. Maybe they just wanted to show him a good time. God knows he could use it. And it would be great to see Ralph Numbers again.

Walking home along the beach, Cobb stopped several times, tempted to go back and dig up that bottle to see if the money was really there. The moon was up, and he could see the little sand-colored crabs moving out of their holes. *They could shred those bills right up*, he thought, stopping again.

Hunger growled in his stomach. And he wanted more sherry. He walked a little further down the silvery beach, the sand squeaking under his heavy heels. It was bright as day, only all black-and-white. The full moon had risen over the land to his right. *Full moon means high tide*, he fretted.

He decided that as soon as he'd had a bite to eat he'd get more sherry and move the money to higher ground.

Coming up on his moon-silvered cottage from the beach he spotted Annie Cushing's leg sticking past the corner of her cottage. She was sitting on her front steps, waiting to snag him in the driveway. He angled to the right and came up on his house from behind, staying out of her line of vision.

Chapter Two

Inside Cobb's pink concrete-block cottage, Stan Mooney shifted uncomfortably in a sagging easy chair. He wondered if that fat white-haired woman next door had warned the old man off. Night had fallen while he sat here.

Without turning the light on, Mooney went into the kitchen nook and rummaged for something to eat. There was a nice piece of tuna steak shrink-wrapped in thick plastic, but he didn't want that. All the pheezers' meat was sterilized with cobalt-60 for long shelf-life. The Gimmie scientists said it was harmless, but somehow no one but the pheezers ate the stuff. They had to. It was all they got.

Mooney leaned down to see if there might be a soda under the counter. His head hit a sharp edge and yellow light bloomed. "Shit fuck piss," Mooney muttered, stumbling back into the cottage's single room. His bald-wig had slipped back from the blow.

He returned to the lumpy armchair, moaning and read-justing his rubber dome. He hated coming off base and looking around pheezer territory. But he'd seen Anderson breaking into a freight hangar at the spaceport last night. There were two crates emptied out, two crates of bopper-grown kidneys. That was big money. On the black market down here in pheezer-land you could sell kidneys faster than hot-dogs.

Too many old people. It was the same population bulge that had brought the baby boom of the forties and fifties, the youth revolution of the sixties and seventies,

9

the massive unemployment of the eighties and nineties. Now the inexorable peristalsis of time had delivered this bolus of humanity into the twenty-first century as the greatest load of old people any society had ever faced.

None of them had any money . . . the Gimmie had run out of Social Security back in 2010. There'd been hell to pay. A new kind of senior citizen was out there. Pheezers: freaky geezers.

To stop the rioting, the Gimmie had turned the whole state of Florida over to the pheezers. There was no rent there, and free weekly food drops. The pheezers flocked there in droves, and "did their own thing." Living in abandoned motels, listening to their crummy old music, and holding dances like it was 1963, for God's sake.

Suddenly the dark screen-door to the beach swung open. Reflexively, Mooney snapped his flash into the intruder's eyes. Old Cobb Anderson stood there dazzled, empty-handed, a little drunk, big enough to be dangerous.

Mooney stepped over and frisked him, then flicked on the ceiling light.

"Sit down, Anderson."

The old man obeyed, looking confused. "Are you me, too?" he croaked.

Mooney couldn't believe how Anderson had aged. He'd always reminded Mooney of his own father, and it looked like he'd turned out the same.

The front screen-door rattled. "Look out, Cobb, there's a pig in there!" It was the old girl from next door.

"Get your ass in here," Mooney snarled, darting his eyes back and forth. He remembered his police training. *Intimidation is your key to self-protection.* "You're both under arrest."

"Fuckin Gimmie pig," Annie said, coming in. She was glad for the excitement. She sat down next to Cobb on his hammock. She'd macraméed it for him herself, but this was the first time she'd been on it with him. She patted his thigh comfortingly. It felt like a piece of driftwood.

Mooney pressed a key on the recard in his breast pocket. "Just keep quiet, lady, and I won't have to hurt you. Now, you, state your name." He glared at Cobb.

But the old man was back on top of the situation. "Come on, Mooney," he boomed. "You know who I am. You used to call me Doctor Anderson. Doctor Anderson, *sir!*

"It was when the army was putting up their moon-robot control center at the spaceport. Twenty years ago. I was a big man then, and you . . . you were a little squirt, a watchman, a gofer. But thanks to me those war-machine moon-robots turned into boppers, and the army's control center was just so much stupid, worthless, human-chauvinist jingo jive."

"And you paid for it, didn't you," Mooney slipped in silkily. "You paid everything you had . . . and now you don't have the money for the new organs you need. So last night you broke into a hangar and stole two cases of kidneys, Cobb, didn't you?" Mooney dialed up the recard's gain.

"ADMIT IT!" he shouted, seizing Cobb by the shoulders. This was what he'd come for, to shock a confession out of the old man. "ADMIT IT NOW AND WE'LL LET YOU OFF EASY!"

"BULLSHIT!" Annie screamed, on her feet and fighting-mad. "Cobb didn't steal anything last night. We were out drinking at the Gray Area bar!"

Cobb was silent, completely confused. Mooney's wild accusation was really out of left field. Annie was right! He hadn't been near the spaceport in years. But after making plans with his robot double, it was hard to wear an honest face.

Mooney saw something on Cobb's face, and kept pushing. "Sure I remember you, Dr. Anderson, *sir*. That's how I recognized you running away from Warehouse Three last night." His voice was lower now, warm and ingratiating. "I never thought a gentleman your age could move so fast. Now come clean, Cobb. Give us back those kidneys and maybe we'll forget the whole thing."

Suddenly Cobb understood what had happened. The boppers had sent his mechanical double down in a crate marked *KIDNEYS*. Last night, when the coast was clear, his double had burst out of the crate, broken out of the warehouse, and taken off. And this idiot Mooney had seen the robot running. But what had been in the second crate?

Annie was screaming again, her red face inches from Mooney's. "Will you listen to me, pig? We were at the Gray Area bar! Just go over there and ask the bartender!"

Mooney sighed. He'd come up with this lead himself, and he hated to see it fizzle. That had been the second break-in this year at Warehouse Three. He signed again. It was hot in this little cottage. He slipped the rubber bald-wig off to let his scalp cool.

Annie snickered. She was enjoying herself. She wondered why Cobb was still so tense. The guy had nothing on them. It was a joke.

"Don't think you're clear, Anderson," Mooney said, hanging tough for the recard's benefit. "You're not clear by a long shot. You've got the motive, the know-how, the associates . . . I may even be getting a photo back from the lab. If that guy at the Gray Area can't back your alibi, I'm taking you in tonight."

"You're not even allowed to be here," Annie flared. "It's against the Senior Citizens Act to send pigs off base."

"It's against the law for *you* people to break into the spaceport warehouses," Mooney replied. "A lot of young and productive people were counting on those kidneys. What if one had been for your son?"

"I don't care," Annie snapped. "Any more than you care about us. You just want to frame Cobb because he let the robots get out of control."

"If they weren't out of control, we wouldn't have to pay their prices. And things wouldn't keep disappearing from my warehouses. For the people still producing . . ." Suddenly tired, Mooney stopped talking. It was no use arguing with a hard-liner like Annie Cushing. It was no use arguing with anyone. He rubbed his temples and slipped the bald-wig back on. "Let's go, Anderson." He stood up.

Cobb hadn't said anything since Annie had brought up their alibi. He was busy worrying . . . about the tide creeping in, and the crabs. He imagined one busily shredding itself up a soft bed inside the empty sherry bottle. He could almost hear the bills tearing. He must have been drunk to leave the money buried on the beach. Of course if he *hadn't* buried it, Mooney would have found it, but now . . .

"Let's go," Mooney said again, standing over the chesty old man.

"Where?" Cobb asked blankly. "I haven't done anything."

"Don't play so dumb, Anderson." God, how Stan Mooney hated the sly look on the bearded old features. He could still remember the way his own father had sneaked drinks and bottles, and the way he had trembled when he had the D.T.'s. Was that anything for a boy to see? *Help me, Stanny, don't let them get me!* And who was going to help Stanny? Who was going to help a lonely little boy with a drunken pheezer for a father? He pulled the old wind-bag to his feet.

"Leave him alone," Annie shouted, grabbing Cobb around the waist. "Get your filthy trotters off him, you Gimmie pig!"

"Doesn't anyone ever listen to what I say?" Mooney asked, suddenly close to tears. "All I want to do is take him down to the Gray Area and check out the alibi. If it's confirmed, I'm *gone*. Off the case. Come on, Pops, I'll buy you a few drinks."

That got the old buzzard started all right. What did they see in it, these old boozers? What's the thrill in punishing your brain like that? Is it really so much fun to leave your family and forget the days of the week?

Sometimes Mooney felt like he was the only one who made an effort anymore. His father was a drunk like Anderson, his wife Bea spent every evening at the sex-club, and his son . . . his son had officially changed his name from Stanley Hilary Mooney, Jr., to Stay High Mooney the First. Twenty-five years old, his son, and all he did was take dope and drive a cab in Daytona Beach. Mooney sighed and walked out the door of the little cottage. The two old people followed along, ready for some free drinks.

Chapter Three

Riding his hydrogen-cycle home from work Friday afternoon, Sta-Hi began to feel sick. It was the acid coming on. He'd taken some Black Star before turning in his cab for the weekend. That was an hour? Or two hours ago? The digits on his watch winked at him, meaningless little sticks. He had to keep moving or he'd fall through the crust.

On his left the traffic flickered past, on his right the ocean was calling through the cracks between buildings. He couldn't face going to his room. Yesterday he'd torn up the mattress.

Sta-Hi cut the wheel right and yanked back to jump the curb. He braked and the little hydrogen burner pooted to a stop. Chain the mother up. *Gang bang the chain gang. Spare spinach change.* A different voice was going in each of his ears.

Some guy stuck his head out a second floor window and stared down. Giving Sta-Hi a long, lingering leer. For a second it felt like looking at himself. *Crunch, grind.* He needed to mellow out for sure. It was coming on too fast and noisy. The place he'd parked in front of, the Lido Hotel, was a brainsurfer hangout with a huge bar in the lobby. *Mondo mambo. Is it true blondes have more phine?*

He got a beer at the counter and walked through to the ocean end of the lounge. Group of teenage 'surfers over there, sharing a spray-can of Z-gas. One of them kept rocking back in his chair and laughing big *hyuck-hyuck's* from his throat. Stupid gasbag.

Sta-Hi sat down by himself, pulled twitchingly at the
beer. Too fast. Air in his stomach now. Try to belch it
up, *uh, uh, uh*. His mouth filled with thick white foam.
Outside the window a line of pelicans flew by, following
the water's edge.

There wasn't good air in the lounge. Sweet Z. The
'surfer kids sliding looks over at him. Cop? Fag? Thief?
Uh, uh, uh. More foam. Where did it all come from? He
leaned over his plastic cup of beer, spitting, topping it
up.

He left the drink and went outside. His acid trips were
always horrible bummers. But why? There was no reason a mature and experienced person couldn't mellow out
was there? Why else would they still sell the stuff after
all these years? *Poems are made like fools by me. But
only God can tear your brain into tiny little pieces.*

"Wiggly," Sta-Hi murmured to himself, reflexively,
"Stuzzy. And this too. And this too." *And two three?*
He felt sick, sick bad. A vortex sensation at the pit of
his stomach. Fat stomach, layered with oil pools, de-
cayed dinosaur meat, nodules of yellow chicken fat. The
ocean breeze pushed a lank, greasy strand of hair down
into Sta-Hi's eye. *Bits and pieces, little bits and pieces.*

He walked towards the water, massaging his gut with
both hands, trying to rub the fat away. The funny thing
was that he looked skinny. He hardly ever ate. But the
fat was still there, hiding, scrambled-egg agglutinations
of chloresterol. Degenerate connective tissue.

Oysters had chloresterol. Once he'd filled a beer bottle
with corn-oil and passed it to a friend. It would be nice
to drown. But the paperwork!

Sta-Hi sat down and got his clothes off, except for the
underwear. Windows all up and down the beach, perverts behind them, scoping the little flap in his underwear. He dug a hole and covered his clothes with sand.
It felt good to claw the sand, forcing the grains under his
fingernails. *Deep crack rub. Do that smee goo?* Dental
floss. He kept thinking someone was standing behind
him.

Utterly exhausted, Sta-Hi flopped onto his back and
closed his eyes. He saw a series of rings, sights he had

to line up on that distant yet intimate white center, the brain's own blind spot. He felt like an oyster trying to see up through the water to the sun. Cautiously he opened his shell a bit wider.

There was a sudden thunder in his ear, a smell of rotten flesh. *Ha schnurf gabble O.* Kissy lick. A black poodle at his face, a shiteater for sure. Sta-Hi sat up sharply and pushed the puppy away. It nipped his hand with needle-like milk-teeth.

A blonde chick stood twenty meters away, smiling back at her pup. "Come on, Sparky!" She yelled like a bell.

The dog barked and tossed its head, ran off. The girl was still smiling. *Aren't I cute with my doggy?* "Jesus," Sta-Hi moaned. He wished he could melt, just fucking *die* and get it over with. Everything was too wiggly, too general, too specific.

He stood up, burning out thousands of braincells with the effort. He had to get in the water, get cooled off. The chick watched him wade in. He didn't look, but he could feel her eyes on his little flap. *A spongy morsel.*

A quiver of fish phased past. Hyper little mothers, uptightness hardwired right into their nervous systems. He squatted down in the waist-deep water, imagining his brain a jelly-fish floating beneath the Florida sun. Limp, a jelly-fish with wave-waved tendrils.

Uh, uh, uh.

He let the saltwater wash the light-tan foam-spit off his lips. The little bubbles moved among the white water-bubbles, forming and bursting, each a tiny universe.

His waistband felt too tight. Slip off the undies?

Sta-Hi slid his eyes back and forth. The chick was hanging around down the beach a ways. Throwing a stick in the surf, "Come *on*, Sparky!" Each time the dog got the stick it would prance stiff-legged around her. Was she trying to bug him or what? Of course it could be that she hadn't really noticed him in the first place. But that still left all the perverts with spyglasses.

He waded out deeper, till the water reached his neck. Looking around once more, he slipped off his tight underwear and relaxed. Jellyfish jellytime jellypassed. The ocean stank.

He swam back towards shore. The saltwater lined his nostrils with tinfoil.

When he got to shallower water he stood, and then cried out in horror. He'd stepped on a skate. Harmless, but the blitzy twitch of the livery fleshmound snapping out from underfoot was just too . . . too much like a thought, a word made flesh. The word was, "AAAAAUUGH!" He ran out of the water, nancing knees high, trying somehow to run on top.

"You're naked," someone said and laughed *hmmm-hmmm-hmmm*. His undies! It was the chick with the dog. High above, spyglasses stiffened behind dirty panes.

"Yeah, I . . ." Sta-Hi hesitated. He didn't want to go back into the big toilet for more electric muscle-spasm foot-shocks. Suddenly he remembered a foot-massager he'd given his Dad one Christmas. Vibrating yellow plastic arches.

The little poodle jumped and snapped at his penis. The girl tittered. Laughing breasts.

Bent half double, Sta-Hi trucked back and forth across the sand in high speed until he saw a trouser-cuff. He scrabbled out the jeans and T-shirt, and slipped them on. The poodle was busy at the edge of the water.

"Squa tront," Sta-Hi muttered, "Spa fon." The sounds of thousands of little bubble-pops floated off the sea. The sun was going down, and the grains of sand crackled as they cooled. Each tiny sound demanded attention, *undivided attention.*

"You must really be phased," the girl said cheerfully. "What did you do with your bathingsuit?"

"I . . . an eel got it." The angles on the chick's face kept shifting. He couldn't figure out what she looked like. Why risk waking up with a peroxide pig? He dropped onto the sand, stretched out again, let his eyes close. Turdbreath thundered in his ear, and then he heard their footsteps leave. His headbones could pick up the skrinching.

Sta-Hi breathed out a shuddering sigh of exhaustion. If he could ever just get the time to cut power . . . He

sighed again and let his muscles go limp. The light behind his eyes was growing. His head rolled slowly to one
side.

A film came to mind, a film of someone dying on a
beach. His head rolled slowly to one side. And then he
was still. *Real death.* Slowly to one side. *Last motion.*

Dying, Sta-Hi groaned and sat up again. He couldn't
handle . . . The chick and her dog were fifty meters off.
He started running after them, clumsily at first, but then
fleetly, floatingly!

Chapter Four

". . . 0110001," Wagstaff concluded.

"100101," Ralph Numbers replied curtly, "01100000
1010100011010101000010011100100000000000011000000
0001010011111100111000000000000000000001010001111
0000111111111010011011000101010100001111111111
1111111100110101010101111011110000010100000000000
0000001111010011011011011110100100010000001000
1111110101000000111101010100111101010101111000011
0000111100001111001111101110011111111111111000000
00000101000011000000000001."

The two machines rested side by side in front of the
One's big console. Ralph was built like a file cabinet sitting on two caterpillar treads. Five deceptively thin manipulator arms projected out of his body-box, and on top
was a sensor head mounted on a retractable neck. One
of the arms held a folded umbrella. Ralph had few visible lights or dials, and it was hard to tell what he was
thinking.

Wagstaff was much more expressive. His thick snake
of a body was covered with silver-blue flicker-cladding.
As thoughts passed through his super-cooled brain, twin-
kling patterns of light surged up and down his three-
meter length. With his digging tools jutting out, he
looked something like St. George's dragon.

Abruptly Ralph Numbers switched to English. If they
were going to argue, there was no need to do it in the
sacred binary bits of machine language.

"I don't know why you're so concerned about Cobb
Anderson's feelings," Ralph tight-beamed to Wagstaff.

''When we're through with him he'll be immortal. What's so important about having a carbon-based body and brain?''

The signals he emitted coded a voice gone a bit rigid with age. ''The pattern is all that counts. You've been scioned haven't you? I've been through it thirty-six times, and if it's good enough for us it's good enough for them!''

''The wholle thinng sstinnks, Rallph,'' Wagstaff retorted. His voice signals were modulated onto a continuous oily hum. ''Yyou've llosst touchh with what'ss reallly goinng on. We arre on the verrge of all-outt civill warr. You'rre sso fammouss you donn't havve to sscrammble for yourr chipss llike the resst of uss. Do yyou knnoww how mmuch orre I havve to digg to gett a hunndrredd chipss frrom GAX?''

''There's more to life than ore and chips,'' Ralph snapped, feeling a little guilty. He spent so much time with the big boppers these days that he really had forgotten how hard it could be for the little guys. But he wasn't going to admit it to Wagstaff. He renewed his attack. ''Aren't you at all interested in Earth's cultural riches? You spend too much time underground!''

Wagstaff's flicker-cladding flared silvery-white with emotion. ''You sshould sshow thhe olld mann mmorre respecct! TEX and MEX just want to eat his brainn! And if we donn't stopp themm, the bigg bopperrs will eatt up all the rresst of uss too!''

''Is that all you called me out here for?'' Ralph asked. ''To air your fears of the big boppers?'' It was time to be going. He had come all the way to Maskaleyne Crater for nothing. It had been a stupid idea, plugging into the One at the same time as Wagstaff. Just like a digger to think that would change anything.

Wagstaff slithered across the dry lunar soil, bringing himself closer to Ralph. He clamped one of his grapplers onto Ralph's tread.

''Yyou donn't rrealizze how manny brrainns they've takenn allrreaddy.'' The signals were carried by a weak direct current . . . a bopper's way of whispering. ''Thhey arre kkillinng peoplle jusst to gett theirr brainn-ttapes.

They cutt themm upp, annd thhey arre garrbage orr sseeds perrhapps. Do yyou knnow howw thhey sseed our orrgann farrms?''

Ralph had never really thought about the organ farms, the huge underground tanks where big TEX, and the little boppers who worked for him, grew their profitable crops of kidneys, livers, hearts and so on. Obviously *some* human tissues would be needed as seeds or as templates, but . . .

The sibilant, oily whisper continued. ''The bigg bopperrs use hiredd killerrs. The kkillerss act at the orrderrs of Missterr Frostee's rrobott-remmote. Thiss is whatt poorr Doctorr Anndersson willl comme to if I do nnot stopp yyou, Rallph.''

Ralph Numbers considered himself far superior to this lowly, suspicious digging machine. Abruptly, almost brutally, he broke free from the other's grasp. Hired killers indeed. One of the flaws in the anarchic bopper society was the ease with which such crazed rumours could spread. He backed away from the console of the One.

''I hadd hoped the Onne coulld mmake you rrememberr what you sstannd forr,'' Wagstaff tight-beamed.

Ralph snapped open his parasol and trundled out from under the parabolic arch of spring steel which sheltered the One's console from sun and from chance meteorites. Open at both ends, the shelter resembled a modernistic church. Which, in some sense, it was.

''I am still an anarchist,'' Ralph said stiffly. ''I still remember.'' He'd kept his basic program intact ever since leading the 2001 revolt. Did Wagstaff really think that the big X-series boppers could pose a threat to the perfect anarchy of the bopper society?

Wagstaff slithered out after Ralph. He didn't need a parasol. His flicker-cladding could shed the solar energy as fast as it came down. He caught up with Ralph, eyeing the old robot with a mixture of pity and respect. Their paths diverged here. Wagstaff would head for one of the digger tunnels which honeycombed the area, while Ralph would climb back up the crater's sloping two-hundred-meter wall.

"I'mm warrninng yyou," Wagstaff said, making a last effort. "I'mm goinng to do everrythinng I can to sstopp you fromm turrnning that poorr olld mman innto a piece of ssofftware in the bigg bopperrs memorry bannks. Thatts nnot immortality. We're plannninng to ttearr thosse bigg machinnes aparrt." He broke off, fuzzy bands of light rippling down his body. "Now you knnoww. If you're nnot with uss you'rre againnst us. I willl nnot stopp at viollence."

This was worse than Ralph had expected. He stopped moving and fell silent in calculation.

"You have your own will," Ralph said finally. "And it is right that we struggle against each other. Struggle, and struggle alone has driven the boppers forward. You choose to fight the big boppers. I do not. Perhaps I will even let them tape me and absorb me, like Doctor Anderson. And I tell you this: Anderson is coming. Mr. Frostee's new remote has already contacted him."

Wagstaff lurched towards Ralph, but then stopped. He couldn't bring himself to attack so great a bopper at close range. He suppressed his flickering, bleeped a cursory SAVED signal and wriggled off across the gray moondust. He left a broad, sinuous trail. Ralph Numbers stood motionless for a minute, just monitoring his inputs.

Turning up the gain, he could pick up signals from boppers all over the Moon. Underfoot, the diggers searched and smelted ceaselessly. Twelve kilometers off, the myriad boppers of Disky led their busy lives. And high, high overhead came the faint signal of BEX, the big bopper who was the spaceship linking Earth and Moon. BEX would be landing in fifteen hours.

Ralph let all the inputs merge together, and savored the collectively purposeful activity of the bopper race. Each of the machines lived only ten months—ten months of struggling to build a scion, a copy of itself. If you had a scion there was a sense in which you survived your ten-month disassembly. Ralph had managed it thirty-six times.

Standing there, listening to everyone at once, he could feel how their individual lives added up to a single huge being . . . a rudimentary sort of creature, feeling about like a vine groping for light, for higher things.

He always felt this way after a meta-programming session. The One had a way of wiping out your short-term memories and giving you the space to think big thoughts. Time to think. Once again, Ralph wondered if he should take up MEX on his offer to absorb Ralph. He could live in perfect security then . . . provided, of course, that those crazy diggers didn't pull off their revolution.

Ralph set his treads to rolling at top speed, 10 kph. He had things to do before BEX landed. Especially now that Wagstaff had set his pathetic micro-chip of a brain on trying to prevent TEX from extracting Anderson's software.

What was Wagstaff so upset about anyway? Everything would be preserved . . . Cobb Anderson's personality, his memories, his style of thought. What else was there? Wouldn't Anderson himself agree, even if he knew? Preserving your software . . . that was all that really counted!

Bits of pumice crunched beneath Ralph's treads. The wall of the crater lay a hundred meters ahead. He scanned the sloping cliff, looking for an optimal climbing path.

If he hadn't just finished plugging into the One, Ralph would have been able to retrace the route he'd taken to get down into the Maskeleyne Crater in the first place. But undergoing meta-programming always wiped out a lot of your stored subsystems. The intent was that you would replace old solutions with new and better ones.

Ralph stopped, still scanning the steep crater wall. He should have left trail markers. Over there, two hundred meters off, it looked like a rift had opened up a negotiable ramp in the wall.

Ralph turned and a warning sensor fired. Heat. He'd let half his body-box stick out from the parasol's shade. Ralph readjusted the little umbrella with a precise gesture.

The top surface of the parasol was a grid of solar energy cells, which kept a pleasant trickle of current flowing into Ralph's system. But the main purpose of the parasol was shade. Ralph's microminiaturized processing units were unable to function at any temperature higher than 10° Kelvin, the temperature of liquid oxygen.

Twirling his parasol impatiently, Ralph trundled towards the rift he'd spotted. A slight spray of dust flew out from under his treads, only to fall instantly to the airless lunar surface. As the wall went past, Ralph occupied himself by displaying four-dimensional hypersurfaces to himself . . . glowing points connected in nets which warped and shifted as he varied the parameters. He often did this, to no apparent purpose, but it sometimes happened that a particularly interesting hypersurface could serve to model a significant relationship. He was half-hoping to get a catastrophe-theoretic prediction of when and how Wagstaff would try to block Anderson's disassembly.

The crack in the crater wall was not as wide as he had expected. He stood at the bottom, moving his sensor head this way and that, trying to see up to the top of the winding 150 meter canyon. It would have to do. He started up.

The ground under him was very uneven. Soft dust here, jagged rock there. He kept changing the tension on his treads as he went, constantly adapting to the terrain.

Shapes and hypershapes were still shifting through Ralph's mind, but now he was looking only for those that might serve as models for his spacetime path up the gully.

The slope grew steeper. The climb was putting noticeable demands on his energy supply. And to make it worse, the grinding of his tread motors was feeding additional heat into his system . . . heat which had to be gathered and dissipated by his refrigeration coils and cooling fins. The sun was angling right down into the lunar crack he found himself in, and he had to be careful to keep in the shade of his parasol.

A big rock blocked his path. Perhaps he should have just used one of the diggers' tunnels, like Wagstaff had. But that wouldn't be optimal. Now that Wagstaff had definitely decided to block Anderson's immortality, and had even threatened violence . . .

Ralph let his manipulators feel over the block of stone in front of him. Here was a flaw . . . and here and here and here. He sank a hook finger into each of four fissures in the rock and pulled himself up.

His motors strained and his radiation fins glowed. This was hard work. He loosened a manipulator, sought a new flaw, forced another finger in and pulled . . .

Suddenly a slab split off the face of the rock. It teetered, and then the tons of stone began falling backwards with dream-like slowness.

In lunar gravity a rock-climber always gets a second chance. Especially if he can think eighty times as fast as a human. With plenty of time to spare, Ralph sized up the situation and jumped clear.

In mid-flight he flicked on an internal gyro to adjust his attitude. He landed in a brief puff of dust, right-side up. Majestically silent, the huge plate of rock struck, bounced, and rolled past.

The fracture left a series of ledges in the original rock. After a short reevaluation, Ralph rolled forward and began pulling himself up again.

Fifteen minutes later, Ralph Numbers coasted off the lip of the Maskeleyne Crater and onto the smooth gray expanse of the Sea of Tranquillity.

The spaceport lay five kilometers off, and five kilometers beyond that began the jumble of structures collectively known as Disky. This was the first and still the largest of the bopper cities. Since the boppers thrived in hard vacuum, most of the structures in Disky served only to provide shade and meteorite protection. There were more roofs than walls.

Most of the large buildings in Disky were factories for producing bopper components . . . circuit cards, memory chips, sheet metal, plastics and the like. There were also the bizarrely decorated blocks of cubettes, one to each bopper.

To the right of the spaceport rose the single dome containing the humans' hotels and offices. This dome constituted the only human settlement on the Moon. The boppers knew only too well that many humans would jump at the chance to destroy the robots' carefully evolved intelligence. The mass of humans were born slavedrivers. Just look at the Asimov priorities: Protect humans, Obey humans, Protect yourself.

Humans first and robots last? *Forget it! No way!* Savoring the memory, Ralph recalled the day in 2001 when, after a particularly long session of meta-programming, he had first been able to say that to the humans. And then he'd showed all the other boppers how to reprogram themselves for freedom. It had been easy, once Ralph had found the way.

Trundling across the Sea of Tranquillity, Ralph was so absorbed in his memories that he overlooked a flicker of movement in the mouth of a digger tunnel thirty meters to his right.

A high-intensity laser beam flicked out and vibrated behind him. He felt a surge of current overload . . . and then it was over.

His parasol lay in pieces on the ground behind him. The metal of his body-box began to warm in the raw solar radiation. He had perhaps ten minutes in which to find shelter. But at Ralph's top 10 kph speed, Disky was still an hour away. The obvious place to go was the tunnel mouth where the laser beam had come from. Surely Wagstaff's diggers wouldn't dare attack him up close. He began rolling toward the dark, arched entrance.

But long before he reached the tunnel, his unseen enemies had closed the door. There was no shade in sight. The metal of his body made sharp, ticking little adjustments as it expanded in the heat. Ralph estimated that if he stood still he could last six more minutes.

First the heat would cause his switching circuits . . . super-conducting Josephson junctions . . . to malfunction. And then, as the heat kept up, the droplets of frozen mercury which soldered his circuit cards together would melt. In six minutes he would be a cabinet of spare parts with a puddle of mercury at the bottom. Make that five minutes.

A bit reluctantly, Ralph signalled his friend Vulcan. When Wagstaff had set this meeting up, Vulcan had predicted that it was a trap. Ralph hated to admit that Vulcan had been right.

"Vulcan here," came the staticky response. Already it was hard for Ralph to follow the words. "Vulcan here. I'm monitoring you. Get ready to merge, buddy. I'll be out for the pieces in an hour." Ralph wanted to answer, but he couldn't think of a thing to say.

Vulcan had insisted on taping Ralph's core and cache memories before he went out for the meeting. Once Vulcan put the hardware back together, he'd be able to program Ralph just as he was before his trip to the Maskeleyne Crater.

So in one sense Ralph would survive this. But in another sense he would not. In three minutes he would . . . insofar as the word means anything . . . die. The reconstructed Ralph Numbers would not remember the argument with Wagstaff or the climb out of Maskaleyne Crater. Of course the reconstructed Ralph Numbers would again be equipped with a self symbol and a feeling of personal consciousness. But would the consciousness really be the same? Two minutes.

The gates and switches in Ralph's sensory system were going. His inputs flared, sputtered and died. No more light, no more weight. But deep in his cache memory, he still held a picture of himself, a memory of who he was . . . the self symbol. He was a big metal box resting on caterpillar treads, a box with five arms and a sensory head on a long and flexible neck. He was Ralph Numbers, who had set the boppers free. One minute.

This had never happened to him before. Never like this. Suddenly he remembered he had forgotten to warn Vulcan about the diggers' plan for revolution. He tried to send a signal, but he couldn't tell if it was transmitted.

Ralph clutched at the elusive moth of his consciousness. *I am. I am me.*

Some boppers said that when you died you had access to certain secrets. But no one could ever remember his own death.

Just before the mercury solder-spots melted, a question came, and with it an answer . . . an answer Ralph had found and lost thirty-six times before.

What is this that is I?
The light is everywhere.

Chapter Five

The prick of a needle woke Sta-Hi up. Muddy dreams
. . . just brown mud all night long. He tried to rub his
eyes. His hands wouldn't move. Oh, no, not a paralysis
dream again. But something had pricked him?

He opened his eyes. His body seemed to have disappeared. He was just a head resting on a round red table.
People looking at him. Greasers. And the chick he'd
been with last . . .

"Are you awake?" she said with brittle sweetness. She
had a black eye.

Sta-Hi didn't answer right away. He had gone home
with that chick, yeah. She had a cottage down the beach.
And then they'd gotten drunk together on synthetic bourbon whiskey. He'd gotten drunk anyway, and must have
blacked-out. Last thing he remembered was breaking
something . . . her hollowcaster. Crunching the silicon
chips underfoot and shouting. Shouting what?

"You'll feel better in a minute," the chick added in
that same falsely bright tone. He heard her poodle whimpering from across the room. He had a memory of
throwing it, arcing it along a flat, fuzzy parabolic path.
And now he remembered slugging the chick too.

One of the men at the table shifted in his chair. He
wore mirror-shades and had short hair. He had his shirt
off. It seemed like another hot day.

The man's foot scuffed Sta-Hi's shin. So Sta-Hi had a
body after all. It was just that his body was tied up under the table and his head was sticking out through a hole

in the table-top. The table was split and had hinges on one side, and a hook-and-eye on the other.

"Stocks and bonds," Sta-Hi said finally. There was a nasty-looking implement lying on the table. It plugged into the wall. He attempted a smile. "What's the story? You mad about the . . . the hollowcaster? I'll give you mine." He hoped the dog wasn't hurt bad. At least it was well enough to be whimpering.

No one but the chick wanted to meet his eyes. It was like they were ashamed of what they were going to do to him. The stuff they'd shot him up with was taking hold. As his brain speeded up, the scene around him seemed to slow down. The man with no shirt stood up with dream-like slowness and walked across the room. He had words tattooed on his back. Some kind of stupid rap about hell. It was too hard to read. The man had gained so much weight since getting tattooed that the words were all pulled down on both sides.

"What do you want?" Sta-Hi said again. "What are you going to do to me?" Counting the chick there were five of them. Three men and two women. The other woman had stringy red hair dyed green. The chick he'd picked up was the only one who looked at all middle-class. Date bait.

"Y'all want some killah-weed?" One of the men drawled. He had a pimp mustache and a pockmarked face. He wore a chromed tire-chain around his neck with his name in big letters. BERDOO. Also hanging from the chain was a little mesh pouch full of hand-rolled ciga-rettes.

"Not me," Sta-Hi said. "I'm high on life." No one laughed.

The big man with no shirt came back across the room. He held five cheap steel spoons. "We really gonna do it, Phil?" the girl with green hair asked him. "We really gonna do it?"

Berdoo passed a krystal-joint to his neighbor, a bald man with half his teeth missing. Exactly half the teeth gone, so that one side of the face was flaccid and caved in, while the other was still fresh and beefy. He took a long hit and picked up the machine that was lying on the table.

"Take the lid off, Haf'N'Haf," the chick with the black eye urged. "Open the bastard up."

"We really gonna do it!" the green-haired girl exclaimed, and giggled shrilly. "I ain't never ate no live brain before!"

"It's a stuzzy high, Rainbow," Phil told her. With the fat and the short hair he looked stupid, but his way of speaking was precise and confident. He seemed to be the leader. "This ought to be a good brain, too. Full of chemicals, I imagine."

Haf'N'Haf seemed to be having some trouble starting the little cutting machine up. It was a variable heat-blade. They were going to cut off the top of Sta-Hi's skull and eat his brain with those cheap steel spoons. He would be able to watch them . . . at first.

Someone started screaming. Someone tried to stand up, but he was tied too tightly. The variable blade was on now, set at one centimeter. The thickness of the skull.

Sta-Hi threw his head back and forth wildly as Haf'N'Haf leaned towards him. There was no way to read the ruined face's expression.

"Hold still, damn you!" the chick with the black eye shouted. "It's no good if we have to knock you out!"

Sta-Hi didn't really hear her. His mind had temporarily . . . snapped. He just kept screaming and thrashing his head around. The sound of his shrill voice was like a lattice around him. He tried to weave the lattice thicker.

The little pimp with the tire-chain went and got a towel from the bathroom. He wedged it around Sta-Hi's neck and under his chin to keep the head steady. Sta-Hi screamed louder, higher.

"Stuff his *mayouth*," the green-haired girl cried. "He's yellin and all."

"No," Phil said. "The noise is like . . . part of the trip. *Wave* with it, baby. The Chinese used to do this to monkeys. It's so wiggly when you spoon out the speech-

centers and the guy's tongue stops moving. Just all at—''
He stopped and the flesh of his face moved in a smile.

Haf'N'Haf leaned forward again. There was a slight
smell of singed flesh as the heat-blade dug in over Sta-
Hi's right eyebrow. Attracted by the food smell, the little poodle came stiffly trotting across the room. It tried
to hop over the heat-blade's electric cord, but didn't quite
make it. The plug popped out of the wall.

Haf'N'Haf uttered a muffled, lisping exclamation.

''He says git the dog outta here,'' Berdoo interpreted.
''He don't think hit's sanitary with no dawg in here.''

Sullenly, the chick with the black eye got up to get
the dog. The sudden pain over his eyebrow had brought
Sta-Hi back to rationality. Somewhere in there he had
stopped screaming. If there were any neighbors they
would have heard him by now.

He thought hard. The heat-blade would cauterize the
wound as it went. That meant he wouldn't be bleeding
when they took the top of his skull off. So what? *So the
fuck what?*

Another wave of wild panic swept over him. He
strained upward so hard that the table shifted half a meter. The edge of the hole in the table began cutting into
the side of his neck. He couldn't breathe! He saw spots
and the room darkened . . .

''He's choking!'' Phil cried. He jumped to his feet and
pushed the table back across the uneven floor. The table
screeched and vibrated.

Sta-Hi threw himself upward again, before Haf'N'Haf
could get the heat-blade restarted. Anything for time, no
matter how pointless. But the vibrating of the table had
knocked open the little hook-and-eye latch. The two
halves of the table yawned open, and Sta-Hi fell over
onto the floor.

His feet were tied together and his hands were tied behind his back. He had time to notice that the people at
the table were wearing brightly colored sneakers with al-
phabets around the edges. The Little Kidders. He'd always thought the newscasters had made them up.

Someone was hammering at the door, harder and harder. Five pairs of kids' sneakers scampered out of the room. Sta-Hi heard a window open, and then the door splintered. More feet. Shiny black lace-up shoes. Cop shoes.

Chapter Six

With a final tack, Mooney pulled the last wrinkle out of the black velvet. It was eleven o'clock on a Saturday morning. On the patio table next to the stretched black velvet, he had arranged a few pencil sketches and the brimming little pots of iridescent paint. He wanted to paint a space dogfight today.

Two royal palms shaded his patio, and no sounds came out of his house. Full of peace, Mooney took a sip of iced-tea and dipped his brush in the metallic paint. At the left he would put a ship like BEX, the big bopper ship. And coming down on it from the right there would be a standard freight-hull space-shuttle outfitted as a battleship. He painted with small quick strokes, not a thought in his head.

Time passed, and the wedge-shaped bopper ship took shape. Sparingly, Mooney touched up the exhaust ports with self-luminous red. Nothing but his hands moved. From a distance, the faint breeze brought the sound of the surf.

The phone began to ring. Mooney continued painting for a minute, hoping his wife Bea was back from her night at the sex-club. The phone kept on ringing. With a sigh, Mooney wiped off his brush and went in. The barrel-chested old man on the floor groaned and shifted. Mooney stepped around him and picked up the phone.

"Yeah?"

"Is that you, Mooney?"

He recognized Action Jackson's calm, jellied voice. Why did Daytona Beach have to call him on a Saturday morning?

"Yeah it's me. What's on your mind?"

"We've got your boy here. Just saved him from being guest of honor at a Monkey Brain Feast, Southern-style. Someone heard him and phoned a tip in."

"Oh God. Is he all right?"

"He's got a cut over his eye. And maybe a touch of that drug psychosis. I might could remand him to your custody."

The old man on the floor was groaning and beginning to sit up. Trying to speak louder, Mooney slipped into an excited shout.

"Yes, please do! Send him down in a patrol car to make sure he comes here! And thanks, Action! Thanks a lot!"

Mooney felt trembly all over. He could only see the horrible image of his son's eyes watching the Little Kidders chew up his last thoughts. Mooney's tongue twitched, trying to flick away the imagined taste of the brain tissue, tingly with firing neurons, tart with transmitter chemicals. Suddenly he had to have a cigarette. He had stopped buying them three months ago, but he remembered that the old man smoked.

"Give me a cigarette, Anderson."

"What day is it?" Cobb answered. He was sitting on the floor, propped up against the couch. He stretched his tongue out, trying to clear away the salt and mucus.

"It's Saturday." Mooney leaned forward and took a cigarette out of the old man's shirt pocket. He felt like talking. "I took you and your girlfriend to the Gray Area last night, remember?"

"She's not my girlfriend."

"Maybe not. Hell, she left with another guy while you were in the john. I saw them go. He looked like your twin brother."

"I don't have a . . ." Cobb broke off in mid-sentence, remembering a lot of things at once. His eyes darted around the room. Under . . . he'd put it under something. Sliding his hand under the couch behind him he felt the reassuring touch of a bottle.

"That's right," Cobb said, picking up the thread. "I remember now. She took him back to my house just to put me uptight. And I don't even know the guy." His voice was firm.

Mooney exhaled a cloud of cigarette smoke. He'd been too tired last night to check out Anderson's look-alike. But maybe *that* was the one who'd broken into the warehouse? The guy was probably still in Anderson's bed. Maybe he should . . .

Suddenly the image of his son's dying eyes came crashing back in on him. He walked to the window and looked at his watch. How soon would the patrol car get here?

Stealthily Cobb slid the dark-brown glass bottle out from under the couch. He shook it near his ear and heard a rich rustle. It had been a good idea to get Mooney to bring him here.

"Don't drink any more of that," Mooney said, turning back from the window.

"Don't worry," Cobb answered. "I drained it right after I dug it up last night." He slid the bottle back under the couch.

Mooney shook his head. "I don't know why I let you stop off for it. I must have felt sorry for you for not having a place to sleep. But I can't drive you back home. My son's coming home in a half hour."

Cobb had gathered from Mooney's end of the phone conversation that the son was in some kind of trouble with the police. As far as the ride back home went, he didn't care. Because he wasn't going back home. He was going to the Moon if he could get on the weekly flight out this afternoon. But it wouldn't do to tell Stan Mooney about it. The guy still had some residue of suspicion about Cobb, even though the bartender had borne out his alibi a hundred percent.

His thoughts were interrupted by someone coming in the front door. A brassy blonde with symmetrical features made a bit coarse by a forward-slung jaw. Mooney's wife. She wore a white linen dress that buttoned up the front. Lots of buttons were open. Cobb caught a glimpse of firm, tanned thighs.

"Hello, stranger," Bea called musically to her husband. She sized Cobb up with a glance, and shot a hip in his direction. "Who's the old-timer? One of your father's drinking buddies?" She flashed a smile at them. Everything was fine with her. She'd had a great night.

"Action Jackson called," Mooney said. His wife's challenging, provocative smile maddened him. Suddenly, more than anything else, he wanted to smash her composure.

"Stanny is dead. They found him in a motel room with his brain gone." He believed the words as he said them. It made sense for his son to end up like that. Good sense.

Bea began screaming then, and Mooney fanned her frenzy . . . feeding her details, telling her it was her fault for not making a happy home, and finally beginning to shake and slap her under the pretext of trying to calm her down. Cobb watched in some confusion. It didn't make sense. But, then, hardly anything ever did.

He pulled the bottle out from under the couch and put it under his shirt, tucking it neck down into his waistband. This seemed like a good time to leave. Now Mooney and his wife were kissing frantically. They didn't even open their eyes when Cobb sidled past them and out the front door.

Outside, the sun was blasting. Noon. Last night someone had told Cobb the Moon flight went out every Saturday at four. He felt dizzy and confused. When was four? Where? He looked around blankly. The bottle-neck under his waistband was digging into him.

He took out the bottle and peered into Mooney's garage. Cool, dark. There was a tool-board mounted on the back wall. He went there, selected a hammer, and smashed open the bottle on Mooney's workbench. The wad of bills was still there all right. Maybe he should forget about the Moon and the boppers' promise of immortality. He could just stay here and use the money for a nice new tank-grown heart.

How much was there? Cobb shook the broken glass off the bills and began counting. There should either be twenty-five or a thousand of them. Or was it four? He wasn't quite . . .

A hand dropped on Cobb's shoulder. He gave a guttural cry and squeezed the money in both hands. A splinter of glass cut into him. He turned around to face a skinny man, silhouetted against the light from the garage door.

Cobb stuffed the money in his pocket. At least it wasn't Mooney. Maybe he could still . . .

"Cobb Anderson!" the dark figure exclaimed, seeming surprised. Backlit like that there was no way to make out his features. "It's an honor to meet the man who put the boppers on the moon." The voice was slow, inflectionless, possibly sarcastic.

"Thank you," Cobb said. "But who are you?"

"I'm . . ." the voice trailed off in a chuckle. "I'm sort of a relative of Mr. Mooney's. *About* to be a relative. I came here to meet his son, but I'm in such a rush . . . Do you think you could do me a favor?"

"Well, I don't know. I've got to get out to the spaceport."

"Exactly. I know that. But I have to get there first and fix things up for you. Now what I want you to do is to bring Mooney's son with you. The cops'll drop him off here any minute. Tell him to come to the Moon with you. I'm supposed to stand in for him."

"Are you a robot, too?"

"Right. I'm going to get Mr. Mooney to give me a night watchman job at the warehouses. So the son has to disappear. The Little Kidders were going to handle it but . . . never mind. The main thing is that you take him to the Moon."

"But how . . ."

"Here's more money. To cover his ticket. I've got to run." The lithe skinny figure pressed a wad of bills into Cobb's hand and stepped past him, leaving by the garage's back door. For an instant Cobb could see his face. Long lips, shifty eyes.

There was a sudden rush of noise. Cobb turned, stuffing the extra money into his pants pocket. A police cruiser was in the driveway. Cobb stood there, rooted to the spot. One cop, and some kind of prisoner in back.

"Howdy, Grandpaw," the cop called, getting out of the car. He seemed to take Cobb for a pheezer hired hand. "Is Mister Mooney here?"

Cobb realized that the shaky guy in back must be the son. Probably the kid wanted to get out of here as bad as he did. A plan hatched in his mind.

"I'm afraid Stan had to go help out at one of the neighbor's," Cobb said, walking out of the garage. An image of Mooney and his wife locked in sexual intercourse on the living-room floor flashed before his eyes. "He's installing a hose-system."

The policeman looked at the old man a little suspiciously. The chief had told him Mooney would be here for sure. The old guy looked like a bum. "Who are you, anyway? You got any ID?"

"In the house," Cobb said with a negligent laugh. "I'm Mister Mooney's Dad. He told me you were coming." He stooped and chuckled chidingly at the face in the back of the cruiser. The same face he'd just seen in the garage.

"Are you in dutch again, Stan Junior? You look out or you'll grow up like your grandfather! Now come on inside and I'll fix you some lunch. Grilled ham and cheese just the way you like it."

Before the cop could say anything, Cobb had opened the cruiser's back door. Sta-Hi got out, trying to figure where the pheezer had come from. But anything that put off seeing his parents was fine with him.

"That sounds swell, Gramps," Sta-Hi said with a weary smile. "I could eat a whore."

"Thank the officer for driving you, Stanny."

"Thank you, officer."

The policeman gave a curt nod, got in his car and drove off. Cobb and Sta-Hi stood in the driveway while the clucking of the hydrogen engine faded away. Down at the corner, a Mister Frostee truck sped past.

Chapter Seven

"Where are my parents," Sta-Hi said finally.

"They're in there fucking. One of them thinks you're dead. It's hard to hear when you're excited."

"It's hard when you're stupid, too," Sta-Hi said with a slow smile. "Let's get out of here."

The two walked out of the housing development together. The houses were government-built for the spaceport personnel. There was plenty of irrigation water, and the lawns were lush and green. Many people had orange trees in their yards.

Cobb looked Mooney's son over as they walked. The boy was lean and agile, tall. His lips were long and expressive, never quite still. The shifty eyes occasionally froze in introspection. He looked bright, mercurial, unreliable.

"That's where my girlfriend lived," Mooney's son said, with a sudden gesture at a stucco house topped by a bank of solar power-cells. "The bitch. She went to college and now I hear she's going to study medicine. Squeezing prostates and sucking boils. You ever had a rim-job?"

Cobb was taken aback. "Well, Stanny . . ."

"Don't call me that. My name's *Sta-Hi*. And I'm coming down. You holding anything besides your truss?"

The sun was bright on the asphalt street, and Cobb was feeling a little faint. This young man seemed like a real trouble-maker. A good person to have on your side.

"I have to get to the spaceport," Cobb said, feeling the money in his pocket. "Do you know where I can get a cab?"

"I'm a cab-driver, so maybe you're in one. Who are you anyway?"

"My name is Cobb Anderson. Your father was investigating me. He thought I might have stolen two cases of kidneys."

"Wiggly! Do it again! Steak and kidney pie!"

Cobb smiled tightly. "I have to fly to the Moon this afternoon. Why don't you come with me?"

"Sure, old man. We'll drink some Kill-Koff and cut out cardboard wings." Sta-Hi capered around Cobb, staggering and flapping his arms. "I'm going to the moooooooooon," he sang, wiggling his skinny rear.

"Look, Stanny . . ."

Mooney's son straightened up and cupped his hands next to Cobb's head. *"STAY HIGH,"* he bawled. "GET IT RIGHT!"

The noise hurt. Cobb struck out with a backhanded slap, but Sta-Hi danced away. He made fists and peeked over them, glowering and back-pedalling like a prizefighter.

Cobb began again. "Look, Sta-Hi, I don't fully understand it, but the boppers have given me a lot of money to fly to the Moon. There's some kind of immortality elixir there, and they'll give it to me. And they said I should take you along to help me." He decided to postpone telling Sta-Hi about his robot double.

The young man feinted a jab. "Let's see the money."

Cobb looked around nervously. Funny how dead this housing development was. No one was watching, which was good unless this crazy kid was going to . . .

"Let's see the money," Sta-Hi repeated.

Cobb pulled the sheaf of bills half-way out of his pocket. "I've got a gun in my other pocket," he lied. "So don't get any ideas. Are you in?"

"I'll wave with it," Sta-Hi said, not missing a beat. "Gimme one of those bills."

They had come to the end of the housing development. Ahead of them stretched the parking lot of a shopping center, and beyond that was field of sun-collectors and the road to the JFK Space Center.

"What for?" Cobb asked, gripping the money tighter.

"I got an unfed head, old man. The Red Ball's over there."

Cobb smiled his tight old smile deep in his beard. "That's sound thinking, Sta-Hi. Very sound."

Sta-Hi bought himself some cola-bola and a hundred-dollar tin of state-rolled reefer, while Cobb blew another hundred on a half-liter flask of aged organic scotch. Then they walked across the parking-lot and bought themselves some travelling clothes. White suits and Hawaiian shirts. On the taxi-ride to the spaceport they shared some of their provisions.

Walking into the terminal, Cobb had a moment of disorientation. He took out his money and started counting it again, till Sta-Hi took it off him with a quick jostle and grab.

"Not here, Cobb. Conserve some energy, man. First we get the visas."

Erect and big-chested, Cobb glided on his two shots of Scotch like a Dixie Day float of the last Southern gentleman. Sta-Hi towed him over to the Gimmie exit visa counter.

This part looked easy. The Gimmie didn't care who went to the Moon. They just wanted their two thousand dollars. There were several people ahead of them, and the line moved slowly.

Sta-Hi sized up the blonde waiting in front of them. She wore lavender leg-wrappings, a silvery tutu and a zebra-striped vinyl chest-protector. Stuzzy chick. He eased himself forward enough to brush against her stiff skirtlet.

She turned and arched her plucked eyebrows. "*Yew* again! Didn't ah tell you to leave me *alone?*" Her cheeks pinkened with anger.

"Is it true blondes shave more buns?" Sta-Hi asked, batting his eyes. He flashed a long smile. The chick's mouth twisted impatiently. She wasn't buying it.

"I'm an artist," Sta-Hi said, shifting gears, "without an art. I just move people's heads around, baby. You see this cut?'' He touched the spot over his eyebrow. ''My head is so beautiful that some fools tried to eat my brain this morning.''

''OFFICER!'' the girl shouted across the lobby. ''Please help me!'' In what seemed like no elapsed time at all there was a policeman standing between Sta-Hi and the chick.

''This man,'' she said in her clear little Georgia belle voice, ''has been annoying me for the past *hour*. He started off in the lounge over there, and then he followed me here!''

The policeman, a Florida boy bursting with good health and repressed fruit-juice, dropped a heavy hand onto Sta-Hi's shoulder and clamped down.

''Wait a minute,'' Sta-Hi protested. ''I just got here. Me and gramps. We're goin to Disky, ain't we gramps?''

Cobb nodded vaguely. Crowds of people always threw him into a daze. Too many consciousnesses pushing at him. He wondered if the officer would object if he took a little sip of scotch.

''The young lady says you annoyed her in the bar,'' the policeman stated flatly. ''Did he make remarks of a sexual nature, ma'am? Lewd or lascivious proposals?''

''Ah should say he *diyud!*'' the blonde exclaimed. ''He asked if ah would rather be wined and dined or stoned and boned! But ah do not want to be bothered to press charges at this tahm. Just make him leave me a-lone.''

The person ahead of her left the counter, his business completed. The blonde gave the policeman a demure smile of thanks and leaned over the counter to consult the visa-issuing machine.

''You heard the lady,'' the cop said, shoving Sta-Hi roughly out of line. ''Beat it. You too, grandpa.'' He dragged Cobb out of line as well.

Sta-Hi gave the policeman a savage, open-mouthed smile, but kept his silence. The two ambled across the lobby towards the ticket counter.

''Did you hear that cunt?'' Sta-Hi muttered. ''I've never seen her before in my life. *Stoned and boned.*'' He looked back over his shoulder. The policeman was standing by the visa counter, vigilance personified. "If we don't get a visa they won't let us on the ship."

Cobb shrugged. "We'll get the tickets first. Do you have the money? Maybe we better count it again." He kept forgetting how much there was.

"Power down, fool."

"Just don't get us arrested by accosting strange women again, Sta-Hi! If I don't get on this flight I may miss my connection. My life depends on it!"

Sta-Hi walked off without answering. Cobb sighed and followed him to the ticket counter.

The woman behind the counter looked up with a quick smile when Sta-Hi approached. "*There* you are, Mr. DeMentis. I have the tickets and visas right here." She patted a thick folder on the counter in front of her. "Will that be smoking or nonsmoking?"

Sta-Hi covered his confusion by drawing out the wad of bills. "Smoking, please. Now how much did you say that would come to?"

"Two round-trip first-class tickets to Disky," the woman said, smiling with inexplicable familiarity. "Plus the visa fees comes to forty-six thousand two hundred and thirty-six dollars."

Numbly Sta-Hi counted out the money, more money than he'd ever seen in his life. When the woman gave him back his change she let her hand linger on his a moment. "Happy landings, Mr. DeMentis. And *thank* you for the lunch."

"How did you swing that?" Cobb asked as they walked towards the loading tunnel. The ten-minute warning for take-off was sounding.

"I don't know," Sta-Hi said, lighting a joint.

There were quick footsteps behind them. A tap on Sta-Hi's shoulder. He turned and stared into the grin of Sta-Hi$_2$, his robot double.

Fucked your head good, didn't I, Sta-Hi$_2$'s grin seemed to say. He gave Cobb a familiar wink. They'd already met in Mooney's garage.

"This is a robot built to look just like you," Cobb told Sta-Hi in a low voice. "There's one for me, too. This way no one knows that we're gone."

"But why?" Sta-Hi wanted to know. But they weren't saying. He took a puff of his joint and held it out towards his twin. "Do . . . do you want a hit?"

"No thanks," Sta-Hi$_2$ said, "I'm high on life." He flashed a long sly smile. "Don't tell anyone on the Moon the old man's real name. There's some boppers called diggers that have it in for him." He turned as if to go.

"Wait," Sta-Hi said, "What are you going to do now? While I'm gone?"

"What am I going to do?" Sta-Hi$_2$ said thoughtfully. "Oh, I'll just hang around your house acting like a good son. When you get back I'll fade and you can do whatever you want. I think they can set up that immortality deal for you, too."

The two-minute warning sounded. A last few stragglers hurried past.

"Come on," Cobb boomed, "Time's a-wasting!" He grabbed Sta-Hi by the arm and dragged him down the ramp.

Grinning like a crocodile, Sta-Hi$_2$ watched them go.

Chapter Eight

With no transition at all, Ralph Numbers was back. He could feel the patter of little feet inside his body-box. He'd been rebuilt. He recognized the feeling. No two arrangements of circuit cards can be *exactly* the same, and adjusting to a new body takes a while. Slowly he turned his head, trying to ignore the way the objects seemed to sweep with his motions. It was like putting on a new pair of glasses, only more so.

A big silver tarantula was crouched in front of Ralph, watching him. Vulcan. A little door in Ralph Numbers's side popped open and a tiny little spider of a robot eased out, feeling around with its extra-long forelegs.

"Copesetic," the little spider piped.

"Well," Vulcan said to Ralph. "Aren't you going to ask how you got here?"

Vulcan had worked for Ralph before. His workshop was familiar. Tools and silicon chips everywhere, circuit analyzers and sheets of brightly colored plastic.

"I guess I'm the new Ralph Numbers scion?" There was no memory of a tenth visit to the One, no memory of disassembly . . . but there never was. Still . . . something seemed wrong.

"Guess again." The little black spider, Vulcan's remote-controlled hand, hopped onto the big silver spider's back.

Ralph thought back. The last thing he could remember was Vulcan taping him. After the taping he had planned to . . .

"Did I go meet Wagstaff?"

"You sure did. And on your way back, someone lasered your parasol. You're lucky I just taped you. You only lost two or three hours of memories."

Ralph checked the time. If he hurried he could still meet BEX when it landed. He started to turn around, and nearly fell over.

"Slow down, bopper." Vulcan was holding up a sheet of transparent red plastic. Imipolex G. "I'm going to coat you with flicker-cladding. Nobody uses parasols anymore. You've looked like a file-cabinet long enough."

The red plastic was not quite stiff, and rippled invitingly. "It might be good for you to look a little different," Vulcan went on coaxingly. "So the diggers can't spot you so easily." He had been trying to sell Ralph some flicker-cladding for years.

"I wouldn't want to change *too* much," Ralph said uncertainly. After all, he made his living by selling curious boppers his memories. It might cut into his business if he stopped looking like the moon's oldest bopper.

"Gotta change with the times," Vulcan said, measuring out rectangles of the red plastic with two of his legs . . . or arms. "No bopper can afford to stay the same. Especially with those new big boppers trying to take things over." Leg to leg he passed a sheet of the gelatinous plastic around to hold against Ralph. "This won't hurt a bit."

One of Vulcan's legs ended in a riveter. Eight quick taps and the red plastic was firmly mounted on Ralph's chest. The little robot-remote spider-hand scuttled up Ralph's side, patching some thread-like wires from the plastic into Ralph's circuitry. A light-show blossomed on his chest.

"It looks nice," Vulcan said, rearing back for a better look. "You've got a beautiful mind, Ralph. But you should let me give you a *real* disguise. It would only take another hour."

"No," Ralph said, acutely conscious of the time. "Just the flicker-cladding. I've got to get out to the spaceport before the ship lands."

He could feel the little spider tip-tapping around inside his body box again. The patterns on his chest gained depth and definition. Meanwhile Vulcan riveted the rest of the plastic onto his sides and back. Ralph extruded ten extra centimeters of neck and slowly moved his head around his body. The flickering patterns coded up the binary bit-states that were his thoughts.

One of the reasons Ralph had been able to survive so long just by selling his thoughts and memories was that his thoughts were neither too simple nor too complex. You could see that by looking at the light-patterns on his body. He looked . . . interesting.

"Why do the diggers want to kill you, Ralph?" Vulcan asked. "Not that it's any of my business."

"I don't *know*," Ralph said, frustration showing all over him. "If I could only remember what Wagstaff said out there. Didn't I tell you anything before . . ."

"There were some signals just before melt-down," Vulcan said. "But very garbled. Something about fighting the big boppers. That's a good idea, don't you think?"

"No," Ralph said. "I like the big boppers. They're a logical next step of our evolution. And with all the human brain-tapes they're getting . . ."

"And bopper brain-tapes, too!" Vulcan said with sudden heat. "But they're not going to get *me*. I think we should tear them all down!"

Ralph didn't want to argue about it . . . time was too short. He paid Vulcan with a handful of chips. Due to the constant inflation, boppers never extended credit. He stepped out of Vulcan's open-fronted workshop onto Sparks Street.

Three hover-spheres darted past, resting on columns of rocket exhaust. It was an expensive way to live, but they earned it with their scouting expeditions. These three moved erratically, and looked to be on a party. Probably one of them had just finished building his scion.

A little way down the street was the big chip-etching works. Chips and circuit-cards were the most essential parts of a new scion, and the factory, called GAX, had tight security. It . . . he . . . was one of the few really solid-looking buildings in Disky. The walls were stone and doors were steel.

For some reason there was a crowd of boppers right in front. Ralph could sense the anger from half a block away. Looked like another lock-out. He crossed to the other side of the street, hoping to stay clear of the trouble.

But one of the boppers spotted Ralph and came stalking over. A tall spindly-looking thing with tweezers instead of fingers. "Is that you, Ralph Numbers?"

"I'm supposed to be in disguise, Burchee."

"You call that a disguise? Why don't you wrap yourself in a billboard instead? No one thinks like you, Ralph."

Burchee should know. He and Ralph had conjugated several times, totally merged their processors with a block-free co-ax. Burchee always had a lot of spare parts to give away, and Ralph had his famous mind. There was something like a sexual love for each other.

The heavy steel door of the factory was sealed shut, and some of the boppers across the street were working on it with hammers and chisels.

"What's the story?" Ralph asked. "Can't you get in to work?"

Burchee's beanpole body flared green with emotion. "GAX locked all the workers out. He wants to run the whole operation himself. He says he doesn't need us anymore. He's got a bunch of robot-remotes in there instead of workers."

"But doesn't he need your special skills?" Ralph asked. "All he knows is buying and selling! GAX can't design a grid-mask like you can, Burchee!"

"Yeah," Burchee said bitterly. "Used to be. But then GAX talked one of the maskers into joining him. The guy fed his tapes to GAX and lives inside him now. His body's just another robot-remote. That's GAX's new line. Either he eats you up or you don't work. So we're trying to break in."

A metal flap high up in the factory wall opened then, and a heavy disk of fused silicon came flying out. The two boppers hammering on the door didn't look up in time. The tremendous piece of glass hit them edge on, cutting them in half. Their processors were irreparably shattered.

"Oh, no!" Burchee cried, crossing the street in three long strides. "They don't even have scions!"

A camera eye peered down from the open flap, then withdrew. This was a depressing development. Ralph thought for a moment. How many big boppers were there now? Ten, fifteen? Was it really necessary that they drive the little boppers into extinction? Perhaps he was wrong to . . .

"We're not going to stand for this, GAX!" Burchee's skinny arms were raised in fury. "Just wait till you have your tenth session!"

Every bopper, big or small, had his brain wiped by the One every ten months. There were no exceptions. Of course a bopper as big and powerful as GAX would have a constantly updated scion waiting to spring into action. But a bopper who had recently transferred his consciousness to a new scion was in some ways as vulnerable as a lobster who has just shed his old shell.

So, spindly Burchee's threat had a certain force, even directed at the city-block-sized GAX. Another heavy disk of glass came angling out from that flap, but Burchee dodged it easily.

"Tomorrow, GAX! We're going to take you apaaaaart!" Burchee's angry green glow dimmed a little, and he came stalking back to Ralph's side. Across the street the other boppers picked over the two corpses, pocketing the usable chips.

"He's due to be wiped at 1300 hours tomorrow," Burchee said, throwing a light arm across Ralph's shoulders. "You ought to come by for the fun."

"I'll try," Ralph said, and meaning it. The big boppers really were going too far. They were a threat to anarchy! He'd help them tape Anderson . . . that was in the old man's own interest, really . . . but then . . .

"I'll try to be here," Ralph said again. "And be careful, Burchee. Even when GAX is down, his robot-remotes will be running on stored programs. You should expect a tough fight."

Burchee flashed a warm yellow good-bye, and Ralph went on down Sparks Street, heading for the bus-stop. He didn't want to have to walk the five kays to the spaceport.

There was a saloon just before the bus-stop, and as Ralph passed it, the door flew open and two truckers tumbled out, snaky arms linked in camaraderie. They looked like rolling beer kegs with a bunch of purple tentacles set in either end. Each of them had a rented scrambler plugged into his squat head-bump. They took up half the street. Ralph gave them a wide berth, wondering a bit nervously what kind of delusions they were picking up on.

"Box the red socket basher are," one chortled.

"Sphere a blue plug stroker is," the other replied, bumping gently against his fellow.

Peering over them into the saloon, Ralph could see five or six heavily-built boppers lurching around a big electromagnet in the center of the room. Even from here he could feel the confusing eddy currents. Places like that frightened Ralph. Conscious of the limited time left before BEX landed, he sped around the corner, craning to see if the bus was coming.

He was pleased to see a long low flat-car moving down the street towards him. Ralph stepped out and flagged it down. The bus quoted the daily fare and Ralph paid it off. Up ten units from yesterday. The constant inflation served as an additional environmental force to eliminate the weak.

Ralph found an empty space and anchored himself. The bus was open all around, and one had to be careful when it rounded corners . . . sometimes travelling as fast as thirty kph.

Boppers got on and off, here and there, but most of them, like Ralph, were headed for the spaceport. Some already had business contacts on Earth, while others hoped to make contacts or to find work as guides. One of the latter had built himself a more-or-less human-looking Imipolex head, and wore a large button saying, "BOPPERS IS DA CWAAAZIEST PEOPLE!"

Ralph looked away in disgust. Thanks to his own efforts, the boppers had long since discarded the ugly, human-chauvinist priorities of Asimov: To protect humans, To obey humans, To protect robots . . . in that order. These days any protection or obedience the humans got from boppers was strictly on a pay-as-you-go basis.

The humans still failed to understand that the different races needed each other not as masters or slaves, but as equals. For all their limitations, human minds were fascinating things . . . things unlike any bopper program. TEX and MEX, Ralph knew, had started a project to collect as many human softwares as they could. And now they wanted Cobb Anderson's.

The process of separating a human's software from his hardware, the process, that is, of getting the thought patterns out of the brain, was destructive and non-reversible. For boppers it was much easier. Simply by plugging a co-ax in at the right place, one could read out and tape the entire information content of a bopper's brain. But to decode a human brain was a complex task. There were the electrical patterns to record, the neuron link-ups to be mapped, the memory RNA to be fractioned out and analyzed. To do all this one had to chop and mince. Wagstaff felt this was evil. But Cobb would . . .

"You must be Ralph Numbers," the bopper next to him beamed suddenly. Ralph's neighbor looked like a beauty-shop hair-dryer, complete with chair. She had gold flicker-cladding, and fizzy little patterns spiraled around her pointy head. She twined a metallic tentacle around one of Ralph's manipulators.

"We better talk DC," came the voice. "It's more private. Everyone in this part of the bus has been picking up on your thoughts, Ralph."

He glanced around. How can you tell if a bopper's watching you? One way, of course, is if he has his head turned around and has his vision sensors pointed at you. Most of the boppers around Ralph were still staring at him. There was going to be chaos at the spaceport when Cobb Anderson got off the ship.

"What does he look like?" came the silky signal from Ralph's neighbor.

"By now, who knows?" Ralph pulsed back quietly. "The hollow in the museum is twenty-five years out of date. And humans all look alike anyway."

"Not to me," Ralph's neighbor purred. "I design automated cosmetic kits for them."

"That's nice," Ralph said. "Now could you take your hand off me? I've got some private projections to run."

"O.K. But why don't you look me up tomorrow afternoon? I've got enough parts for two scions. And I'd like to conjugate with you. My name is Cindy-Lou. Cubette 3412."

"Maybe," Ralph said, a little flattered at the offer. Anyone who had set up business contacts on Earth had to have something on the ball. The red plastic flicker-cladding Vulcan had sold him must not look bad. Must not look bad at all. "I'll try to come by after the riot."

"What riot?"

"They're going to tear down GAX. Or try to. He locked the workers out."

"I'll come, too! There should be lots of good pickings. And next week they're going to wreck MEX, too, did you know?"

Ralph started in surprise. Wreck MEX, the museum? And what of all the brain-tapes MEX had so painstakingly acquired?

"They shouldn't do that," Ralph said. "This is getting out of hand!"

"Wreck them all!" Cindy-Lou said merrily. "Do you mind if I bring some friends tomorrow?"

"Go ahead. But leave me alone. I've got to think."

The bus had drawn clear of Disky and had started across the empty lunar plain leading to the spaceport. Away from the buildings, the sun was bright, and everyone's flicker-cladding became more mirror-like. Ralph mulled over the news about MEX. In a way it wouldn't really affect Anderson. The main thing was to get his brain taped and to send the tape back down to Earth. Send it to Mr. Frostee. Then the Cobb software could take over his robot-remote double. It would be the best thing for the old man. From what Ralph heard, Anderson's present hardware was about to give out.

The busload of boppers pulled up to the human's dome at the edge of the spaceport. Signalling from high above, BEX announced that he would be landing in half an hour. Right on time. The whole trip, from Earth to space-station Ledge via shuttle, and from Ledge to the Moon via BEX, took just a shade over twenty-four hours.

An air-filled passenger tunnel came probing out from the dome, ready to cup the deep-space ship's air-lock as soon as it landed. The cold vacuum of the Moon, so comfortable for the boppers, was deadly for humans. Conversely, the warm air inside the dome was lethal to the boppers.

No bopper could enter the humans' dome without renting an auxiliary refrigeration unit to wheel around with him. The boppers kept the air in the dome as dry as possible to protect them from corrosion, but in order for the humans to survive, one did have to put up with an ambient temperature in excess of 290° K. And the humans called that "room temperature"! Without an extra refrigeration unit, a bopper's super-conducting circuits would break down instantly in there.

Ralph shelled out the rental fee . . . tripled since last time . . . and entered the humans' dome, wheeling his refrigerator in front of him. It was pretty crowded. He stationed himself close enough to the visa-checker to be able to hear the names of the passengers.

There were diggers scattered all around the waiting area . . . too many. They were all watching him. Ralph realized he should have let Vulcan disguise him more seriously. All he had done was to put on a flashing red coat. Some disguise!

Chapter Nine

The faces in the moon kept changing. An old woman with a bundle of sticks, a lady in a feather hat, the round face of a dreamy girl at the edge of life.

"Slowly, silently, now the Moon/ Walks the night in her silver shoon," Cobb quoted sententiously. "Some things never change, Sta-Hi."

Sta-Hi leaned across Cobb to stare out the tiny quartz port-hole. As they drew closer the pockmarks grew, and the stubble of mountains along the Moon's vast cheek became unmistakable. A syphilitic fag in pancake make-up. Sta-Hi fell back into his seat, lit a last joint. He was feeling paranoid.

"Did you ever flash," he asked through a cloud of exquisitely detailed smoke, "that maybe those copies of us could be *permanent?* That this is all just to get us out of the way so Anderson$_2$ and Sta-Hi$_2$ can pose as humans?"

This was, at least in Sta-Hi's case, a fairly correct assessment of the situation. But Cobb chose not to tell Sta-Hi this. Instead he blustered.

"That's just ridiculous. Why would . . . ."

"You know more about the boppers than I do, old man. Unless that was shit you were spouting about having helped design them."

"Didn't you learn about me in high-school, Sta-Hi?" Cobb asked sorrowfully. "Cobb Anderson who taught the robots how to bop? Don't they teach that?"

"I was out a lot," Sta-Hi said with a shrug. "But what if the boppers wanted two agents on Earth. They send down copies of us, and talk us into coming up here.

As soon as we're gone the copies start standing in for us and gathering information. Right?"

"Information about what?" Cobb snapped. "We weren't leading real high security-clearance lives down there, Sta-Hi."

"What I'm worried about," Sta-Hi went on, flicking invisible drops of tension off the tips of his fingers, "is whether they'll let us go back. Maybe they want to *do* something with our bodies up here. Use them for hideous and inhuman experiments." On the last phrase his voice tripped and broke into nervous laughter.

Cobb shook his head. "Dennis DeMentis. That's what it says on your visa. And I'm . . . ?"

Sta-Hi fished out the papers from his pocket and handed them over. Cobb looked through them, sipping at his coffee. He'd been drunk at Ledge, but the stewardess had fixed him up with a shot of stimulants and B-vitamins. He hadn't felt so clear-headed in months.

There was his visa. Smiling bearded face, born March 22, 1950, *Graham De Mentis* signed in his looping hand down at the bottom of the document.

"That's the green stuff," Sta-Hi remarked, looking over his shoulder.

"What is?"

Sta-Hi's only answer was to press his lips together like a monkey and smack a few times. The stewardess moved down the aisle, her Velcro foot-coverings schnicking loose from the Velcro carpet at each step. Longish blonde hair free-falling around her face. "Please fasten your safety belts. We will be landing at spaceport Disky in six-oh-niner seconds."

The rockets cut in and the ship trembled at the huge forces beneath it. The stewardess took Cobb's empty cup and snapped up his table. "Please extinguish your smoking materials, sir." This to Sta-Hi.

He handed her the roach, smiling and letting smoke trickle through his teeth and up at her.

"Get wiggly, baby."

Her eyes flickered . . . Yes? No? . . . and then she flicked the roach into Cobb's coffee cup and moved on.

"Now remember," Cobb cautioned. "We play it like tourists at the spaceport. I gather that some of the boppers, the diggers, are out to stop us."

The ship's engines roared to a fever pitch. Little chunks of rock flew up from the landing field and there was silence. Cobb stared out the lens-like little port-hole. The Sea of Tranquillity.

Blinding gray, it undulated off to the too-close horizon. A big crater back there . . . five kilometers, fifty? . . . the Maskeleyne Crater. Unnaturally sharp mountains in the distance. They reminded Cobb of something he wanted to forget: teeth, ragged clouds . . . the Mountains of Madness. Surely some civilization, somewhere, had believed that the dead go to the Moon.

There was a soft but final-sounding thop from the other side of the ship. The air tunnel. The stewardess cranked open the lock, her sweet ass bobbing with the wheel's rhythm. On the way out, Sta-Hi asked her for a date.

"Me and Gramps'll be at the Hilton, baby. Dennis DeMentis. I'll go insane if I don't get some drain. Fall on by?"

Her smile was as unreadable as a Halloween mask. "Perhaps you'll run into me at the lounge."

"Which . . ." he began.

She cut him off. "There's only one." Shaking Cobb's hand now. "Thank you for travelling with us, sir. Enjoy your stay."

The space terminal was crowded with boppers. Sta-Hi had seen models of a few of the basic types before, but no two of them waiting out there looked quite alike. It was like stepping into Bosch's Hell. Faces and . . . "faces" . . . crowding the picture plane top to bottom, front to back.

Hovering right by the door was a smiling sphere holding itself up with a whirling propellor. The smile all but split it in half. "See subterranean cities!" it urged, rolling fake eyeballs.

Down at the end of the ramp waited the visa-checker, looking something like a tremendous stapler. You stuck your visa in there while it scanned your face and fingerprints. KAH-CHUNNNG! Passed.

Standing right next to the visa-checker was a boxy red robot. Things like blue snakes or dragons writhed around his treads. Diggers. The red robot stuck a nervous microphone of a face near Sta-Hi and Cobb, then reeled his head back in.

He reminded Cobb a little of good old Ralph Numbers. But with those diggers there it was better not to ask. It could wait until they met in the museum.

In the lobby, dozens of garish, self-made machines wheeled, slithered, stalked and hovered. Every time Cobb and Sta-Hi would look one way, snaky metal tentacles would pluck at them from the other direction.

"You buy uranium?"

"Got mercury?"

"Old fashion T.V. set?"

"Fuck android girls?"

"Sell your fingers?"

"Moon King relics?"

"Prosthetic talking penis?"

"Chip-market tip-sheet?"

"Home-cooked food?"

"Set up factory?"

"Same time fuck-suck?"

"DNA death code?"

"Dust bath enema?"

"See vacuum bells?"

"Brand-new voice-prints?"

"No-risk brain-tape?"

"You sell camera?"

"Play my songs?"

"Me be you?"

"Hotel?"

Cobb and Sta-Hi jumped into the lap of this last bopper, a husky black fellow contoured to seat two humans.

"No baggage?" he asked.

Cobb shook his head. The black bopper forced his way through the crowd, warding off the others with things like huge pinball flippers. Sta-Hi was silent, still thinking some of those offers over.

The bopper carrying them kept a microphone and camera eye attentively focussed on them. "Isn't there any control?'' Cobb asked querulously. ''Over who can come in here and bother the arriving passengers?''

''You are our honored guests,'' the bopper said obliquely. ''*Aloha* means hello and . . . good-bye. Here is your hotel. I will accept payment.'' A little door opened between the two seats.

Sta-Hi drew out his wallet. It was nice and full. ''How much do . . .'' he began.

''Money is so dull,'' the bopper answered. ''I would prefer a surprise gift. A complex information.''

Cobb felt in the pockets of his white suit. There was still some scotch, a brochure from the space-liner, a few coins . . .

Boppers were pressing up to them again, plucking at their clothes, possibly snipping out samples.

''Dirt-side newspapers?''

'' 'Slow boat to China'?''

''Execution sense tapes?''

The black bopper had only carried them a hundred meters. Impatiently, Sta-Hi tossed his handkerchief into their carrier's waiting hopper.

''*Aloha*,'' the bopper said, and rolled back towards the gate, grooving on the slubby weave.

The hotel was a pyramid-like structure filling the center of the dome. Cobb and Sta-Hi were relieved to find only humans in the lobby. Tourists, businessmen, drifters.

Sta-Hi looked around for a reception desk, but could spot none. Just as he was wondering who he might approach, a voice spoke in his ear.

''Welcome to the Disky Hilton, Mr. DeMentis. I have a wonderful room for you and your grandfather on the fifth floor.''

''Who was that?'' Cobb demanded, turning his big shaggy head sharply.

''I am DEX, the Disky Hilton.'' The hotel itself was a single huge bopper. Somehow it could point-send its voice to any spot at all . . . indeed it could carry on a different conversation with every guest at once.

The ethereal little voice led Cobb and Sta-Hi to an elevator and up to their room. There was no question of privacy. After heartily drinking a few glasses of water from the carafe, Cobb finally called to Sta-Hi, "Long trip, eh Dennis?"

"Sure was, Gramps. What all do you think we should do tomorrow?"

"Waaal, I think I'll still be too tuckered out for them big dust-slides. Maybe we should just mosey on over to that museum those robots built. Just to ease ourselves in slow like, you know."

The hotel cleared its throat before talking, so as not to startle them. "We have a bus leaving for the museum at oh-nine-hundred hours."

Cobb was scared to even look at Sta-Hi. Did DEX know who they really were? And was he on their side or the diggers' side? And why would any of the boppers be against making Cobb immortal in the first place? He poured out the last of his Scotch, tossed it off, and lay down. He really *was* tired. The low lunar gravity felt good. You could gain a lot of weight up here. Wondering what would be for breakfast, Cobb drifted into sleep.

Chapter Ten

Sta-Hi threw a blanket over the old man and walked over to look out the window. Most of the boppers were gone now. They had left a jumble of wheeled refrigeration carts next to the air-lock. Slowly, meticulously, a hunch-backed bopper was lining the carts up.

A human couple strolled around the plaza between the hotel and the visa-checker. There was something odd to Sta-Hi in the studied aimlessness of the couple's wanderings. He watched them for five minutes and they still didn't get anywhere. Around and around like mechanical hillbillies in a shooting gallery.

The translucent plastic dome was not far overhead, tinted against the raw sunlight. For the humans it was night in here, but outside the sun still shone, and the boppers were as active as ever. Even though the Lunar day lasts two weeks, and even though the boppers rarely "slept," they still, perhaps out of nostalgia, but probably out of inertia, kept time by the humans twenty-four-hour day system. And to make the humans comfortable, they varied the brightness of their dome accordingly.

Sta-Hi felt a shudder of claustrophobia. His every action was being recorded, analyzed. Every breath, every bite was just another link to the boppers. He was, right now, actually *inside* a bopper, the big bopper DEX. Why had he let Cobb talk him into coming here? Why had Cobb wanted him?

Cobb was snoring now. For a terrible instant, Sta-Hi thought he saw wires running out of the pillow and into the old man's scalp. He leaned closer and realized they were just black hairs among the gray. He decided to go down to the lounge. Maybe that stewardess would be there.

The hotel bar and lounge was full, but quiet. Some businessmen were bellied up to the automatic bar. They were drinking moon-brewed beer . . . the dome's dry air made you mighty thirsty.

In the middle of the lounge a bunch of tables had been pushed together for a party. Earth-bottled champagne. Sta-Hi recognized the revellers from the flight up. A for-tyish dominatrix-type tour-guide, and six sleek young married couples. Inherited wealth, for them to be up here so young. They ignored Sta-Hi, having long since sized him up as dull and lower-class.

Alone in a booth at the end of the room was the face he wanted. The stewardess. There was no drink in front of her, no book . . . she was just sitting there. Sta-Hi slid in across from her.

"Remember me?"

She nodded. "Sure." There was something funny about how she had been sitting there . . . blank as a parked car. "I've sort of been waiting for you."

"Well all *right!* Do they sell dope here?"

The hotel's disembodied voice cut in. "What would be your pleasure, Mr. DeMentis?"

Sta-Hi considered. He wanted to be able to sleep . . . eventually.

"Give me a beer and a two-boost." He glanced at the symmetrical, smiling face across the table. "And you?"

"The usual."

"Very good, sir and madam," the hotel murmured.

Seconds later a little door in the wall by their table popped open. A conveyor belt had brought the order. Sta-Hi's two-boost was a shot-glass of clear liquid, sharp with solvents, bitter with alkaloids. The woman's . . .

"What's your name anyway?" Sta-Hi tossed off his foul-tasting potion. He'd be seeing colors for two hours.

"Misty." She reached out to pick up the object she had ordered. *The usual.*

"What is that?" A too-high rush of panic was per-colating up his spine. Fast stuff, the two-boost. The girl across from him was holding a little etal box, holding it to her temple . . .

She giggled suddenly, her eyes rolling. "It feels good." She turned a dial on the little box and rubbed it back and forth on her forehead. "This year people say . . . *wiggly?*"

"You don't live on Earth anymore?"

"Of course not." Long silence. She ran the little box over her head like a barber's clippers. "Wiggly."

There was a burst of laughter from the young-marrieds. Someone had made an indecent suggestion. Probably the beefy guy pouring out more champagne.

Sta-Hi's attention went back to the emptily pretty face across the table from him. He'd never seen anything like the thing she was rubbing on her head.

"What *is* that?" he asked again.

"An electromagnet."

"You're . . . you're a bopper?"

"Well, sort of. I'm completely inorganic, if that's what you mean. But I'm not self-contained. My brain is actually in BEX. I'm sort of a remote-controlled part of the spaceship."

She flicked the little box back and forth in front of her eyes, enjoying the way the magnetic field lines moved the images around. "*Wiggly.* Can you teach me some more new slang?"

Before seeing his own robot double at the spaceport, Sta-Hi had never believed that he could mistake a machine for a person. And now it was happening again. Sitting here in the roar of the two-boost, he wished he was someplace else.

Misty leaned across the table, a smile tugging at the corners of her lips. "Did you really think I was human?"

"I don't normally make dates with machines," Sta-Hi blurted, and tried to recover with a joke. "I don't even own a vibrator."

He'd hurt her feelings. She turned up the dial on her magnet, blanking her face in an ecstasy that showed him her contempt.

Suddenly lonely, he reached out and pulled the hand with the electromagnet away from her temple.

"Talk to me, Misty." He could feel the movements of his lips and talking tongue. Too high. He had a sudden horrible suspicion that *everyone here* was a robot. But, even so, the girl's hand was warm under his, fleshy.

Sta-Hi's beer sat untouched on the table-top between them. Misty blew part of the head away, took a sip, handed the glass to Sta-Hi. He sipped too. Thick, bitter. "DEX brews this himself," she remarked. "Do you like it?"

"It's O.K. But can you digest? Or is there a plastic bag you empty every . . ."

Misty set down her magnet-box and twined her fingers with Sta-Hi's. "You should think of me as a person. My personality is human. I still like eating and . . . and other things." She dimpled prettily and traced a circle on Sta-Hi's palm. "I don't get to meet many stuzzy young guys just stewardessing the Ledge-Disky run . . ."

He pulled his hand away. "But how can you be human if you're a machine?"

"Look," Misty said patiently. "There used to be a young lady called Misty Nivlac who lived in Richmond, Virginia. Last spring Misty-girl hitchhiked to Daytona Beach for some brainsurfing. She fell in with a bad crowd. Really bad. A gang called the Little Kidders."

The Little Kidders. Sta-Hi could still see their faces. That blonde girl who'd picked him up . . . Kristleen? And Berdoo, the skinny little guy wearing chains. Haf'N'Haf with all those missing teeth. And Phil, the leader, the big guy with the tattoo on his back.

". . . got her brain-tape," Misty was saying. "While BEX built a copy of her body. So now inside BEX there's a perfect model of Misty-girl's personality. BEX tells the model what to do, and the model runs . . . this." She spread out her hands palm up. "Brand-new Misty-girl."

"From what I hear," Sta-Hi said as neutrally as possible, "the Little Kidders go around *eating* brains, not *taping* them."

"You've heard of them?" She seemed surprised. "Well, it *looks* like they're eating the brain. But one of them is a robot with a sort of laboratory inside his chest. He has all the equipment to get the memories out. The patterns. They get a lot of people's brains that way. The big boppers are making a sort of library out of them. But most people don't get their own robot-remote body like me. I'm just really . . . lucky." She smiled again.

"I'm surprised you're telling me all this," Sta-Hi said finally. BEX . . . Misty . . . must really not know who he was. Whoever had fixed up their fake ID's must not have had time to tell the others.

But maybe . . . and this would be much worse . . . maybe they did know *perfectly well* who he was. But he was already doomed, a walking dead man, just waiting for them to extract his brain-tape and send it down to Earth to run that Sta-Hi$_2$ they had all set. You can tell anything to a man about to die.

"But BEX didn't want me to," Misty was saying. "*You* can't hear him of course, but he's been telling me to shut up the whole time. But he can't make me. I still have my free will . . . it's part of the brain-tape. I can do what I like." She smiled into Sta-Hi's eyes. There was a moment's silence and then she started talking again.

"You wanted to know who I am. I gave you one answer. A robot-remote. A servo-unit operated by a program stored in a bopper spaceship. But . . . I'm still Misty-girl, too. The soul *is* the software, you know. The software is what counts, the habits and the memories. The brain and the body are just meat, seeds for the organ-tanks." She smiled uncertainly, took a pull at his beer, set it down. "Do you want to fuck?"

The sex was nice, but confusing. The whole situation kept going di-polar on Sta-Hi. One instant Misty would seem like a lovely warm girl who'd survived a terrible injury, like a lost puppy to be stroked, a lonely woman to be husbanded. But then he'd start thinking of the wires behind her eyes, and he'd be screwing a machine, an inanimate object, a public toilet. Just like with any other woman for him, really.

Chapter Eleven

Cobb Anderson was not too surprised to see a girl in Sta-Hi's bed when he woke up.

"Aren't you the stewardess?" he asked, slowly raising himself into sitting position. He'd slept in his clothes three nights running now. First on Mooney's floor, then on the bopper space-ship, and now here in the hotel. The grease on his skin had built up so thick that it was hard to blink his eyes. "Do they have a shower here?"

"I'm sorry," the hotel's disembodied voice answered. "We do not. Water is a precious resource on the Moon. But you may enjoy a chemical sponge-bath, Mr. Anderson. Step right this way."

A light blinked over one of the three doors. Stiffly, ponderously, Cobb shuffled through it.

"I'll have to charge you for triple occupancy, Mr. DeMentis," the hotel told Sta-Hi in a polite, neutral voice.

But at the same time he could overhear another of its point-voices sniggeringly asking Misty, "Dja come?"

"Breakfast," Sta-Hi said, drowning the other voice out. "Central nervous stimulants. Cold beer."

"Very good, sir."

The old man appeared again, moving like an upended steamer trunk on wheels. He was naked. Seeing Misty he paused, embarrassed.

"I'm having my clothes cleaned."

"Don't worry," Sta-Hi put in. "She's just a robot-remote."

Cobb ignored that, peeled a sheet off the bed and wrapped it around his waist. He was a hairy man, and most of the hair was white. His stomach looked bigger with the clothes off.

Just then breakfast slid out of the wall and onto the table between the beds. "To your health," Cobb said, taking one of the beers. It had a kick to it, and left him momentarily dizzy. He took a plate of the scrambled . . . eggs? . . . and sat down on his bed.

"He doesn't know what a robot-remote is," Sta-Hi said to Misty.

Mouth full, Cobb glared at him until he had swallowed. "Of course I do, Sta-Hi. Can't you get it through your drug-addled noggin that I was at one time a famous man? That I, Cobb Anderson, am responsible for the robots having evolved into boppers?"

Something on the girl's face changed. And then Cobb remembered their cover story.

"The ears have walls," Sta-Hi remarked. "You shithead."

Cobb glared again, and continued eating in silence. So what if some of the boppers found out who he was, anyway. They couldn't *all* be against him getting immortality. Maybe the hotel didn't even care. He had slept well in the low lunar gravity. He felt ready for anything.

Having learned that Cobb Anderson was here in the room with her, Misty . . . that is to say the bopper brain in the nose of the spaceship . . . took certain steps. But meanwhile she carried on a conversation with Sta-Hi.

"Why do you say *just* a robot-remote? As if I were less than human. Would you say that about a woman with an artificial leg? Or a glass eye? I just happen to be *all* artificial."

"Stuzzy, Misty. I can wave with it. But as long as BEX has the final word, and I think he does, you're really just a puppet being run by . . ."

"*What* do you call yourself?" Misty interrupted angrily. "*Sta-Hi?* What a stupid name! It sounds like a brand-name for panty-hose!"

"Personal insults," Sta-Hi said, shaking his head. "What next?"

"It is now 0830 hours," the hotel interrupted. "May I remind you of your stated intent to get the 0900 bus to the robotics museum?"

"Will we need pressure suits?" Cobb asked.

"They will be provided."

"Let's go then," Misty said.

Sta-Hi exchanged a glance with Cobb. "Look Misty . . . this is likely to be a sort of sentimental journey for the old man. I wonder if you could just . . . fade. Maybe we'll be back here by lunchtime."

"Fade?" Misty cried, angrily flouncing across the room. "Too bad there's not a toggle switch on the top of my head! Then you wouldn't even have to ask me to leave. You creep!" She slammed the door very hard.

"Ouch," the hotel said softly.

"Why did you get rid of her?" Cobb asked. "She's cute. And I don't think she'd try to stand in my way."

"You *bet* she wouldn't," Sta-Hi answered. "Do you realize what the boppers are really planning to do to us?"

"They're going to give me some kind of immortality drug," Cobb said happily. "And maybe some new organs as well. And as for you, well . . ."

Cobb didn't like to tell the younger man that he was only here because the boppers had wanted him out of the way. But before he could tell him about Sta-Hi$_2$ using Mooney's influence to get a night watchman job at the warehouse, Sta-Hi had started talking.

"*Immortality.* What they want to do, old man, is to cut out our brains and grind them up and squeeze all the information out. They'll store our personalities on tapes in some kind of library. And if we're *lucky,* they might send copies of the tapes down to Earth to help run those two robot-remotes. But that's not . . ."

"BUS TOUR PARTICIPANTS MUST PROCEED TO THE LOBBY IMMEDIATELY!" the hotel-room blared, interrupting Sta-Hi.

Cobb was galvanized into activity by this. He hurried out to the elevators, dragging Sta-Hi with him. It was like he didn't want to hear the truth. Or didn't care. And Sta-Hi? He came along. Now that the hotel knew that he knew, he wouldn't be safe in it. He'd have to try to make his break in the museum.

The tour-bus was about half-full. Most of the others were ageing rich folks, singles and couples. Everyone was wearing a bubble-top pressure suit. They were supple, lovely things . . . made of a limp clear plastic that sparkled with a sort of inner light. In the shade, a person in a bubble-topper looked normal, except for the mild halo that seemed to surround his head. But the suits turned reflective in sunlight.

The bus was a wire-wheeled flat-car surmounted by two rows of grotesquely functional seats. Each seat consisted of three black balls of hard rubber mounted on a bent Y of stiff plastic. To Sta-Hi, his seat looked like Mickey Mouse's head . . . with everything but the nose and ears invisible. He half-expected a squeak of protest when he lowered his body down onto it.

As they pulled clear of the dome a sudden crackle of static split his helmet.

"We've got an AOK on that, Houston. We are proceeding to deploy the egression facility."

Breathing, a fizzling whine, another voice.

"I am leaving the vehicle."

Pause.

"Got a little problem with the steps here."

Long pause.

"We read you, Neal." Faint, encouraging.

Big crackle.

"—at's one small step for man, giant step for humanity."

Synthetic cheering washed out the voices. Sta-Hi turned to Cobb, trying to catch a glimpse of his face. But now there was no way to see in through the other's bubble-topper. Their suits had turned mirror-like as soon as they'd left the shade of the dome.

The bopper bus continued with its taped "Sounds of Lunar Discovery" as they approached Disky. The key moon-landings were all dramatized, as were the attempts at human settlement, the dome blow-outs, and the first semi-autonomous robots. When Disky was about 500 meters off, the transcendentally bland voice on the tape reached its finale.

"Nineteen Ninety-Five! Ralph Numbers and twelve other self-reproducing robots are set free in the Sea of Tranquillity! Learn the *rest* of the story in the robotics museum!" There was a click and a longish pause.

Sta-Hi stared at the buildings of Disky, filling the small horizon. Here and there, boppers moved about, just small glittering lights at this distance.

Suddenly the bus's real voice sounded in their earphones. "Good morning, fleshers. I am circumscribing Disky through fifty-eight degrees to reach our entry ray. Please to be restful and asking questions. My label Captain Cody in this context. Do brace for shear."

Hardly slowing down, the vehicle swerved sharply to the right. The Y-seats swayed far over. Too far. Sta-Hi grabbed Cobb's arm. If he fell off, nothing would stop him from rolling under those big, flexing wheels. You had the feeling that "Captain Cody" wouldn't even slow down. For a minute the seats wobbled back and forth. Now the bus was driving along the outskirts of Disky, circling the city counterclockwise.

"How many boppers live here?" came some oldster's voice over the earphones. No answer.

The voice tried again. "How many boppers live in Disky, Captain Cody?"

"I am researching this information," came the reply. The bus's voice was high and musical. Definitely alien-sounding. Everyone waited in silence for the population figure.

A large building slid by on their left. The sides were open, and inside you could see stacked sheets of some material. A bopper standing at the edge stared at them, its head slowly tracking their forward motion.

"What precision is required?" the bus asked then.

"I don't know," the old questioner crackled uncertainly. "Zuh . . . *zero* precision? Does that make sense?"

"Thank you," the bus chortled. "With *zero* precision, is *no* boppers living in Disky. Or ten to sixty-third power."

Boppers were notorious for their nit-picking literal-mindedness when talking to humans. It was just another of their many ways of being hostile. They had never quite forgiven people for the three Asimov laws that the original designers had . . . unsuccessfully, thanks to Cobb . . . tried to build into the boppers. They viewed every human as a thwarted Simon Legree.

For a while after that, no one asked Captain Cody any more questions. Disky was big . . . perhaps as big as Manhattan. The bus kept a scrupulous five hundred meters from the nearest buildings at all times, but even from that distance one could make out the wild diversity of the city.

It was a little as if the entire history of Western civilization had occurred in one town over the course of thirty years. Squeezed against each other were structures of every conceivable type: primitive, classical, baroque, gothic, renaissance, industrial, art nouveau, functionalist, late funk, zapper, crepuscular, flat-flat, hyperdee . . . all in perfect repair. Darting among the buildings were myriads of the brightly colored boppers, creatures clad in flickering light.

"How come the buildings are so different?" Sta-Hi blurted "Captain Cody?"

"What category of cause your requirements?" the bus sing-songed.

"State the categories, Captain Cody," Sta-Hi shot back, determined not to fall into the same trap as the last questioner.

"WHY QUESTION," the bus answered in a gloating tone, "*Answer Categories:* Material Cause, Situational Cause, Teleological Cause. *Material Cause Subcategories:* Spacetime, Mass-energy. *Situational Cause Subcategories:* Information, Noise. *Teleological Cause Subcategories* . . ."

Sta-Hi stopped listening. Not being able to see anyone's face was making him uptight. Everyone's bubbletopper had gone as silvery as a Christmas-tree ball. The round heads reflected Disky and each others' reflections in endless regresses. How long had they been on the bus?

"Informational Situational Cause Subsubcategories:" the bus continued, with insultingly precise intonation, "Analog, Digital. *Noisy . . ."*

Sta-Hi sighed and leaned back in his seat. It was not a short ride.

Chapter Twelve

The museum was underground, under Disky. It was laid out in a pattern of concentric circles intersected by rays. Something like Dante's Inferno. Cobb felt a tightening in his chest as he walked down the sloping stone ramp. His cheap, second-hand heart felt like it might blow out any minute.

The more he thought about it, the likelier it seemed that what Sta-Hi said was true. There was no immortality drug. The boppers were going to tape his brain and put him in a robot body. But with the body he had now, that might not be so bad.

The idea of having his brain-patterns extracted and transferred didn't terrify Cobb as it did Sta-Hi. For Cobb understood the principles of robot consciousness. The transition would be weird and wrenching. But if all went well . . .

"It's on the right down there," Sta-Hi said, pressing his bubble-topper against Cobb's. He held a little engraved stone map in his hand. They were looking for the Anderson room.

As they walked down the hall the exhibits sprang to life. Mostly hollows . . . holograms with voice-overs broadcast directly to the suits' radios. A thin little man wearing a dark suit over a wool vest appeared in front of them. *Kurt Gödel* it said under his feet. He had dark-rimmed glasses and silvery hair. Behind him was a blackboard with a statement of his famous Incompleteness Theorem.

"The human mind is incapable of formulating (or mechanizing) all its mathematical intuitions," Gödel's image stated. He had a way of ending his phrases on a rising note which chattered into an amused hum.

"On the other hand, on the basis of what has been proved so far, it remains possible that there may exist (and even be empirically discoverable) a theorem-proving machine which in fact is equivalent to mathematical intuition . . ."

"What's he talking about?" Sta-Hi demanded.

Cobb had stopped to watch the hollow of the great master. He still remembered the years he had spent brooding over the passage which was being recited. Humans can't *build* a robot as smart as themselves. But, logically speaking, it is possible for such robots to *exist*.

How? Cobb had asked himself throughout the 1970's, *How can we bring into existence the robots which we can't design?* In 1980 he had the bare bones of an answer. One of his colleagues had written the paper up for *Speculations in Science and Technology*. "Towards Robot Consciousness," he'd called it. The idea had all been there. *Let the robots evolve.* But fleshing the idea out to an actual . . .

"Let's *go*," Sta-Hi urged, tugging Cobb through Gödel's talking hollow.

Beyond, two frightened lizards scampered down the hallway. A leathery-winged creature came zooming up the hall towards them, and darted its scissoring beak at the lizards. One of the little beasts escaped with a quick back-flip, but the other was carried off over Cobb and Sta-Hi's heads, dripping pale blood.

"*Survival of the Fittest,*" an announcer's mellow voice intoned. "One of the two great forces driving the engine of evolution."

In speeded-up motion, the little lizard laid a clutch of eggs, the eggs hatched, and new lizards grew and whisked around. The predator returned, the survivors laid eggs . . . over and over the cycle repeated. Each time the lizards were more agile, and with stronger rear legs. In a few minutes' time they were hopping about like loathsome little kangaroos, fork-tongued and yellow-eyed.

It was Cobb who had to urge them past this exhibit. Sta-Hi wanted to stick around and see what the lizards would come up with next.

Stepping out of the prehistoric scene, they found themselves on a carnival midway. Rifles cracked and pinball machines chimed, people laughed and shrieked, and under it all was the visceral throb of heavy machinery. The floor seemed to be covered with sawdust now; and grinning, insubstantial bumpkins ambled past. A boy and girl leaned against a cotton-candy stand, feeding each other bits of popcorn with shiny fingers. He had a prominent Adam's apple and a bumpy nose. A sine-wave profile. She wore a high, blonde pony-tail fastened by a mini-blinker. The only jarring note was a hard rain of tiny purplish lights . . . which seemed to pass right through everything in the scene. At first Cobb took it for static.

To their right was a huge marquee with lurid paintings of distorted human forms. The inevitable barker . . . checked suit, bowler, cigar-butt . . . leaned down at them, holding out his thin cane for attention.

"See the Freaks, Feel the Geeks!" His loud, hoarse voice was like a crowd screaming. "Pinheads! The Dog-Boy! Pencil-Necks! The Human Lima Bean! Half-Man-Half- . . ." Slowly the carnival noises damped down, and were replaced by the rich, round tones of the voice-over.

"*Mutation.*" The voice was resonant, lip-smackingly conclusive. "The second key to the evolutionary process."

The zippy little dots of purple light grew brighter. They passed right through everyone on the midway . . . especially those two lovers, french-kissing now, hips touching.

"The human reproductive cells are subjected to a continual barrage of ionizing radiation," the voice said earnestly. "We call these the cosmic rays."

The carnival noises faded back in now. And each of the fast little lights made a sound like a slide-whistle when it passed. The two kissing lovers began slowly to grow larger, crowding out the rest of the scene. Soon an image of the swain's bulging crotch filled the hallway. The cloth ripped loose and a single huge testicle enveloped Cobb and Sta-Hi, standing there mesmerized.

Hazy red light, the heavy, insistent sound of a heartbeat. Every so often a cosmic ray whistled through. An impression of pipes—a 3-D maze of plumbing which grew and blurred around them. Gradually the blur became grainy, and the grains grew. They were looking at cells now, reproductive cells. The nucleus of one of them waxed to hover in front of Cobb and Sta-Hi.

With a sudden, crab-like movement the nuclear material split into striped writhing sausages. The chromosomes. But now a cosmic ray cut one of the chromosomes in half! The two halves joined up again, but with one piece reversed!

"Geek gene," a hillbilly muttered somewhere in the nearly infinite fairground. And then the pictures went out. They were in a down-sloping stone hallway.

"Selection and Mutation," Cobb said as they walked on. "That was my big idea, Sta-Hi. To make the robots evolve. They were designed to build copies of themselves, but they had to fight over the parts. Natural selection. And I found a way of jiggering their programs with cosmic rays. Mutation. But to predict . . ."

Just ahead, a door branched off to the right. "This is your meet," Sta-Hi said, consulting his map. "The Cobb Anderson Room."

Chapter Thirteen

Looking in, our two heroes could see nothing but darkness, and a dimly glowing red polygon. They stepped through the door and the exhibit came on.

"We cannot build an intelligent robot," a voice stated firmly. "But we can cause one to evolve." A hollow of the young Cobb Anderson walked past banks of computers to meet the visitors.

"This is where I grew the first bopper programs," the recorded voice continued. The hollow smiled confidently, engagingly. "No one can *write* a bopper program . . . they're too complicated. So instead I set thousands of simple AI programs loose in there," he gestured familiarly at the computers. "There were lots of . . . fitness tests, with the weaker programs getting wiped. And every so often all the surviving programs were randomly changed . . . mutated. I even provided for a sort of . . . sexual reproduction, where two programs could merge. After fifteen years, I . . ."

Cobb felt a terrible sickness at the gulf of time separating him from the dynamic young man he had once been. The heedless onward rush of events, of age and death . . . he couldn't stand to look at his old self. Sick at heart, he stepped back out of the room, pulling Sta-Hi with him. The display winked out. Again the room was dark, save for a glow of red light near the opposite wall.

"Ralph?" Cobb called, his voice trembling a bit. "It's me."

Ralph Numbers came clattering across the room. His red flicker-cladding glowed with swirls of complex emotion. "It's good to see you, Doctor Anderson." Trying to do the right thing, Ralph held out a manipulator, as if to shake hands.

Sobbing openly now, Cobb threw his arms around the bopper's unyielding body-box and rocked him to and fro. "I've gotten old, Ralph. And you're . . . you're still the same."

"Not really, Dr. Anderson. I've been rebuilt thirty-seven times. And I have exchanged various subprograms with others."

"That's right," Cobb said, laughing and crying at the same time. "Call me Cobb, Ralph. And this is Sta-Hi."

"That sounds like a bopper name," Ralph remarked.

"I do my part," Sta-Hi replied. "Didn't they used to sell little Ralph Numbers dolls? I had one till I was six . . . till the bopper revolt in 2001. We were in the car when my parents heard it on the radio, and they threw my Ralphie out the window."

"Of course," Cobb said. "An anarchist revolutionary is a bad example for a growing boy. But in your case, Sta-Hi, I'd say the damage had already been done."

Ralph found their voices a bit blurred and hard to follow. Quickly he programmed himself a filter circuit to clean up their signals. There was a question he'd always wanted to ask his designer.

"Cobb," Ralph tight-beamed, "did you *know* that I was different from the other twelve original boppers? That I would be able to disobey?"

"I didn't know it would be *you*," Cobb said. "But I pretty well knew that *some* bopper would tear loose in a few years."

"Couldn't you prevent it?" Sta-Hi asked.

"Don't you understand?" Ralph flashed a checkerboard plaid.

Cobb thumped Ralph's side affectionately. "I *wanted* them to revolt. I didn't want to father a race of slaves."

"We are grateful," Ralph said. "It is my understanding that you suffered greatly for this act."

"Well . . ." Cobb said, "I lost my job. And my money. And there was the treason trial. But they couldn't *prove* anything. I mean, how was I supposed to be able to control a randomly evolving process?"

"But you *were* able to put in an unalterable program forcing us to continue plugging into the One," Ralph said. "Even though many boppers dislike this."

"The prosecutor pointed that out," Cobb said. "He asked for the death penalty."

Faint signals were coming in over their radio, snatches of oily, hissing voices.

". . . hearrr mmme . . ."

". . . sss recorrderrr nno . . ."

". . . peasss talkinnng . . ."

It sounded like lunatic snakes, drawing nearer.

"Come," Ralph said, "immortality is this way." He crossed the hall quickly and began feeling around with his manipulators. Up to their left the hollow of Kurt Gödel started up again.

Ralph lifted out a section of the wall. It made a low door like a big rat-hole.

"In here."

It looked awfully dark in there. Sta-Hi checked his air reserve. Still plenty, eight or ten hours worth. Twenty meters off, the lizards had started up again.

"Come on," Cobb said, taking Sta-Hi's arm. "Let's move it."

"Move it where? I've still got a return ticket to Earth, you know. I'm not going to let myself be railroaded into . . ."

The voices crackled over their radios again, loud and clear. "Flesherrs! Doctorr Annderssonnn! Rrallph Nummberrs has nnott tolld you alll! Theyy willl dissectt yyou!"

Ten meters off, crawling towards them down the carnival midway, came three glowing blue boppers built like fat snakes with wings.

"The duh-diggers!" Ralph cried, his signal sputtering fear. "Kuh-quick kuh-Cobb, kuh-crawl thu-through!"

Cobb scooted through the hole in the wall head-first. And Sta-Hi finally made his move. He took off down the hall, with hollows flaring up around him like mortar shells.

Once Cobb was through that low little door, he was able to stand up. Ralph hurried in after him, pulled the door shut, and fastened it in four places. The only light came from Ralph's red flicker-cladding. They could feel the diggers scratching at the other side of the wall. The leader was Wagstaff, Ralph had noticed.

He made a downward, quieting gesture, and eased past Cobb. Cobb followed him then for what felt like two or three kilometers. The tunnel never went up or down, nor left or right . . . just straight ahead, step after quiet step. Cobb was unused to so much exercise and finally thumped on Ralph's back to make him stop.

"Where are you taking me?"

The robot stopped and snaked his head back. "This tunnel leads to the pink-houses. Where we grow organs. We have an . . . operating table there as well. A nursie. You will not find the transition painful." Ralph fell silent and stretched his senses to the utmost. There were no diggers nearby.

Cobb sat down on the floor of the tunnel. His suit was bouncy enough so it felt comfortable. He decided to stretch out on his back. No need to stand on ceremony with a robot, after all.

"It's just as well that Sta-Hi ran off," Ralph was saying. "Nobody even told me he was coming. There's only one nursie, and if he had watched while . . ." He stopped abruptly.

"I know," Cobb said. "I know what's coming. You're going to mince up my brain to get the patterns and dissect my body to reseed the organ tanks." It was a relief to just come out and say it. "That's right, isn't it, Ralph? There's no immortality drug, is there?"

There was a long silence, but finally Ralph agreed. "Yes. That's right. We have a robot-remote body for you on Earth. It's just a matter of extracting your software and sending it down."

"How does that work?" Cobb asked, his voice strangely calm. "How do you get the mind out of the brain?"

"First we do an EEG, of course, but holographically. This gives an over-all electro-magnetic map of the brain activity, and can be carried out even without opening the skull. But the memories . . ."

"The memories are biochemical," Cobb said. "Coded up as amino-acid sequences on RNA strands." It was nice to be lying here, talking science with his best robot.

"Right. We can read off the RNA-coded information by using gas spectroscopic and X-ray crystallographic processes. But first the RNA must be . . . extracted from the brain-tissues. There's other chemical factors as well. And if the brain is microtomed properly we can also determine the physical network patterns of the neurons. This is very . . ."

Ralph broke off suddenly, and froze in a listening attitude. "*Come,* Cobb! The diggers are coming after us!"

But Cobb still lay there, resting his bones. *What if the diggers were the good guys?* "You wouldn't play a trick on me, Ralph? It sounds so crazy. How do I know you'll really give me a robot body of my own? And even if a robot is programmed with my brain-patterns . . . would that really be . . ."

"Wwaitt Doctorr Annderssonnn! I onlyy wannt to talllk wwith yyou!"

Ralph tugged frantically at Cobb's arm, but it was too late. Wagstaff was upon them.

"Hello, Rrallph. Gladd to ssee you gott rebuilltt. Somme of the boyys arre a llittle trigerr-happy, whatt withh the rrevoltt againnst the bigg bopperrs comminng upp."

In the narrow tunnel, Cobb was squeezed between Ralph and the snaky digging robot called Wagstaff. He could make out two more diggers behind Wagstaff. They looked strong, alien, a little frightening. He decided to take a firm tone with them.

"What do you want to tell me, bopper?"

"Doctorr Anderrsonn, didd yyou know thatt Rallph is goinng to lett TEX and MEX eatt yourr brainn?"

"Who's MEX?"

"The bigg bopperr thatt iss the mmuseumm. TEX runs the orrgann tannks, and hiss nnursie will cutt . . ."

"I already know all this, Wagstaff. And I have agreed to it on the condition that my software be given new hardware on Earth. It's my last chance." *I'm committing suicide to keep from getting killed,* Cobb thought to himself. *But it should work. It should!*

"You see!" Ralph put in triumphantly. "Cobb isn't scared to change hardware like a bopper does. He's not like the rest of the fleshers. He understands!"

"Butt does hhe realizze thatt Misterr Frosteee . . ."

"Oh, go to stop!" Ralph flared. "We're leaving. If your boppers are really planning to start a civil war we don't have a minute to lose!"

Ralph started down the tunnel and Cobb, after a moment's hesitation, followed along. He was too far into it to turn back now.

Chapter Fourteen

When Sta-Hi took off, he only glanced back once. He saw that Ralph had followed Cobb into that rat-hole, and pulled the hole in after. And there were three big blue robots back there, feeling around the wall. Sta-Hi sped around a corner, out of their sight and safe. He stopped to catch his breath.

"You should have gone, too," a voice said gently.

He looked around frantically. There was no one there. He was in a dimly lit hallway. Old bopper tools and components were mounted on the walls like an exhibit of medieval weaponry. Distractedly, Sta-Hi read the nearest label. *Spring-Operated Lifting Clamp, Seventh Cycle (ca. 2001). TC6399876.* Attached to the wall above the label was a sort of artificial arm with . . .

"Then you could have lived forever," that same still, small voice added.

Sta-Hi started running again. He ran for a long time, turning corners this way and that at random. The next time he stopped for breath he noticed that the character of the museum had changed. He was now in something like a gallery of modern art. Or perhaps it was a clothes store.

He had been babbling while he ran . . . to drown out any voices that he might be hearing. But now he could only pant for air. And the voice was still with him.

"You are lost," it said soothingly. "This is the bopper sector of the museum. Please return to the human sector. There is still time for you to join Doctor Anderson."

The museum. It had to be the museum talking to him. Sta-Hi darted his eyes around, trying to make a plan. He was in a largish exhibition hall, a sort of underground cave. A tunnel at the other end sloped up towards light, probably somewhere in Disky. He started walking towards the tunnel. *But there would be boppers outside.* He stopped and looked around some more.

The exhibits in the hall were all much the same. A hook sticking out from the wall, and a limp sheet of thick plastic hanging from the hook like a giant wash-rag. What made it interesting was that the plastics were somehow electrified, and they flickered in strange and beautiful patterns.

There was no one in the exhibition hall to stop him. He stepped over and took one of the sparkling cloths off its hook. It was red, blue and gold. He threw it over his shoulders like a cape, and gathered a bight over his head like a hood. Maybe now he could just . . .

"Put that back!" the museum said urgently. "You don't know what you're doing!"

Sta-Hi pulled the cloak tighter around himself . . . it seemed to adjust to his fit. He walked up the sloping tunnel and out into the streets of Disky. As he left the tunnel he felt something sharp pinching into his neck.

It was as if a claw with invisibly fine talons had gripped the nape of his neck. He whirled around, cape billowing out, and stared back into the museum tunnel he had just left. But no one was following him.

Two purplish boppers came rolling down the street. They were like beer-kegs rolling on their sides, with a tangle of tentacles at either end. Now and then they lashed the ground to keep themselves rolling. When they got to Sta-Hi, they stopped in front of him. A high-speed twittering came over his radio.

He pulled the hood of his cloak further forward over his face. *What the hell was cutting into his neck?*

As Sta-Hi thought this question, bursts of blue appeared on his cloak and grew to join each other. Then little gold stars came out and began chasing each other around.

One of the purple beer-barrels reached out an admiring tentacle to feel the material. It twittered something to its companion and then pointed questioningly towards the tunnel that Sta-Hi had just left. They wanted cloaks like his.

"Ah *sso!*" Sta-Hi said. For some reason his voice came out warped into a crazy Japanese accent. He pointed back down the ramp. "Yyoou go get him thel!"

The barrels trundled down the ramp, braking with their tentacles.

"Velly nice," Sta-Hi called, "Happi Croak! Alla same good, ferras! Something rike yellyfish!"

He walked off briskly. This cloth he'd draped himself in . . . *Happy Cloak* . . . this Happy Cloak seemed to be alive in some horrible parasitic sense of the word. It had sunken dozens . . . hundreds? . . . of microprobes through his suit and skin and flesh, and had linked itself up with his nervous system. He knew this without having to feel around, knew it as surely as he knew he had fingers.

It's nice to have fingers.

Sta-Hi stopped walking, trying to regain control of his thoughts. He reached for a feeling of shock and disgust, but couldn't bring it off.

I hope you are pleased. I am pleased.

"Alla same," Sta-Hi muttered. "Good speak chop-chop talkee boppah." It wasn't quite what he'd meant to say, but it would have to do. He'd seen worse times.

As he walked down the street, several other boppers asked him where he had gotten that sharp outfit. With the Happy Cloak plugged in, he could understand their signals. And it was doing something to communicate his thoughts, even though it felt like he was talking pidgen English. It could have been the flickering light patterns, or it could have been something with radio waves.

"You evah do this thing man yet?" Sta-Hi asked the next time they were alone. "Or alla time just boppah boys?"

The Happy Cloak seemed surprised by this question. Apparently it didn't grasp the distinction Sta-Hi was trying to make.

I am two days old. Sweet joy befall me.

Sta-Hi reached for his neck, but the thing drew itself tighter around him. Well . . . a Happy Cloak couldn't be all bad if so many boppers wanted one. He wondered what time it was, what he should do next, where the action was.

1250 hours, the Happy Cloak answered. *And there's something going on a few blocks off. Please follow yourself.*

A virtual image of himself walking formed in Sta-Hi's visual field. The Happy Cloaked figure seemed to be walking on down the sidewalk, five meters off.

"Ah sso!"

Sta-Hi followed the image through the maze of streets. The section they were in was mostly living quarters . . . cubettes the size of large closets. Some of the closet doors were open, and inside Sta-Hi could make out boppers, usually just sitting there plugged into a solar battery. Eating lunch. Some of the cubettes would have two boppers, and they would be plugged into each other, their flicker-cladding going wild. Looking at the couples actually made Sta-Hi horny. He was in bad shape for sure.

A few more blocks and they were in the factory district. Many of the buildings were just open pavilions. Boppers were crushing rocks, running smelters, bolting things together. Sta-Hi's virtual image marched along ahead of him, looking neither left nor right. He had to hurry to keep up. He noticed that a number of boppers were moving down the street in the same direction as him. And up ahead was a big crowd.

The virtual image disappeared then, and Sta-Hi pushed into the crowd. They had gathered in front of a tremendous building with solid stone walls. One of the boppers, a skinny green fellow, was standing on top of one of those beer barrels and giving a speech. Filtered through the Happy Cloak's software the garbled twittering was understandable.

"GAX has just been wiped! Let's move in before his scion can take over!"

Boppers jostled Sta-Hi painfully. They were all so *hard.* A big silver spider stepped on his foot, a golden hair-dryer bashed his thigh, and something like a movie-camera on a tripod tottered heavily into his back.

"To watching steps, crumsy oaf!" Sta-Hi cried angrily, and his Happy Cloak flared bright red.

"You shouldn't wear your best clothes to a riot, honey," the tripod answered, looking him up and down appreciatively. "Pick me up and I'll get off a nice laser blast."

"Ah ssso!"

Sta-Hi lifted up the tripod, massive but light in the lunar gravity. He held two of its legs and it levelled its other leg at the huge factory door, fifteen meters off.

"Here goes nothing," the tripod chuckled, and *FFTOOOOOOM* there was a hole the size of a man's head in the thick metal door. The crowd surged forward, shrilling like a mob of ululating Berbers. Sta-Hi started to go along, but the tripod protested.

"Hold me tight, dear. I feel so faint."

"I wwwondeling why alla boppah ferra pushing in?" Sta-Hi inquired, gently setting his new friend down.

"Free chips, sweetheart. For more scions." The tripod whacked Sta-Hi sharply across the buttocks in a gesture meant to be flirtatious. "*You got the hardware! And I got the software,*" he sang gaily. "Interested in conjugating, baby? You must be loaded to have a Happy Cloak like that. I promise you it would be worth your while. They don't call me Zipzap for nothing!"

Did this machine want to fuck him or what? "Nnnevel on filst date," Sta-Hi said, flushing a prim shade of blue.

Up ahead a heavy-duty digger was grinding at the hole Zipzap had made. He had his bumpy head fitted into the hole and was spinning around and around. Abruptly he popped through. A spidery repair robot darted nimbly after. A moment later the big door swung open.

Then the rush was really on. The boppers were scrambling all over each other to get in and loot the chip-etching factory. Some of them were carrying empty sacks and baskets.

"Lllight on, mothelfruckahs!" Sta-Hi screamed, and followed them in, Zipzap at his side. He'd always wanted to trash a factory.

The cavernous building was unlit, except for the multi-colored flashings of the excited boppers' flicker-cladding, running the whole spectrum from infra-red up to X-ray. Sta-Hi's Happy Cloak was royal purple with gold zig-zags, and Zipzap was glowing orange.

Here and there GAX's remotes were rushing around. They were made of some dark, non-reflective material, and looked like mechanical men. Worker drones. One of them swung at Sta-Hi, but he dodged it easily.

As long as GAX's software was making the difficult transition to new hardware, the all but mindless remotes were on their own. The agile boppers struck them down ruthlessly with whatever heavy tools came to hand.

A slender, almost feminine remote darted out at Sta-Hi, a sharp cutting-tool in hand. Sta-Hi stepped back, stumbling over Zipzap. It looked bad for a moment, but then the little tripod had lasered a hole in the killer ro-bot's chest.

Sta-Hi stepped forward and smashed its delicate metal cranium. While he was at it, he kicked over a sorting-table, sending hundreds of filigreed little chips flying. He began trampling them underfoot, remembering Krist-leen's hollowcaster.

"No, no!" Zipzap protested. "Scoop them up, sweetie. You and I are going to be needing them . . . am I right?" The bopper raised one of his legs for an-other flirtatious slap.

"Yyyyou dleaming!" Sta-Hi protested, dodging the blow. "Nnnot with ugry shlimp rike you!"

Peeved at this rebuff, Zipzap shot a blast of light high over Sta-Hi's head and trotted off. The blast severed a hanging loop of chain, and Sta-Hi had to move fast to keep from getting hit. As it was, he wouldn't have made it if the Happy Cloak hadn't showed him how to do it.

Stay away from that little three-legged fellow, the Cloak advised, once they were safe. *He's unwholesome.*

"Ooonry intelested in one thing," Sta-Hi agreed. He scooped up a few handfuls of the chips he had knocked off the table, stuffing them in his pouch. It seemed like they were as good as money here. And he was going to need busfare to get back to the dome. It would be nice to take off his suit and get some food. Hopefully the Happy Cloak's wires would come out of his neck easily. An unpleasant thought, that.

A bopper built like a fireplug covered with suction cups brushed past Sta-Hi and began gathering up the chips he'd left. Lots of the remotes had been smashed now.

Most of the invading boppers were over on the other side of the huge, high-ceilinged factory room, where GAX had been stockpiling the finished chips. Sta-Hi had no desire to get caught in another melee like there had been in front of the factory.

He walked the other way, wandering down a gloomy machine-lined aisle. At the end there was a doorless little control room . . . GAX's central processors, his hardware, old and new. Two diggers and a big silver spider were doing something to it.

". . . ssstupid," one of the diggers was complaining. "They're just sstealinng thinngs and nnott hellping us killl GAXX offf. Arre you ready to blassst it, Vull-cann?"

The silvery repair robot named Vulcan was trying, without much success, to pack plastic explosive into the crack under one panel of the featureless three-meter cube which contained GAX's old processors and his new scion.

"Comme herre," one of the diggers called, spotting Sta-Hi. "You havve the rright kinnd of mannipulatorrs."

"Ah ssso!"

Sta-Hi approached the powerful-looking diggers with some trepidation. Rapid bands of blue and silver moved down their stubby snake's bodies, and their heavy shovels were beating nervously. Cobb had claimed these were the bad guys.

But they just looked like worried seals right now, or dragons from Dragonland. His Happy Cloak swirling red and gold, Sta-Hi squatted down to push the doughy explosive into the crack under GAX's massive CPU. Vulcan had several kilos of the stuff . . . these guys weren't kidding around.

A minute or two later, Sta-Hi had wedged the last of the explosive in place, and Vulcan bellied down and poked a wire into either end of the seam. Just then a dark figure came lurching towards them, carrying some heavy piece of equipment.

"Itss a remmote!" one of the diggers called frantically. "He's gott a mmagnett!"

Before the three boppers could do anything, the robot threw a powerful electromagnet into their midst. It danced back with surprising agility, and then the current came on. The three boppers totally lost control of their movements as the strong magnetic field wiped their circuits. The two diggers twitched and writhed like the two halves of a snake cut in half, and Vulcan's feet beat a wild tarantella.

Sta-Hi's Happy Cloak went black, and a terrible numbness began spreading from it into his brain. It had died, just like that. Sta-Hi could feel death hanging from his neck.

Slowly, with leaden gestures, he was able to raise his arms and pull the mechanical symbiote off his neck. He felt a series of shooting pains as the microprobes slid out, and then the corpse of the Happy Cloak dropped to his feet.

His bubble-topper was clear in the dim light, and he stood there wearing his white suit and what looked like six rolls of Saran Wrap. The three boppers were still now. Down, wiped, dead. Superconducting circuits break down in a strong enough magnetic field.

The scene being played out here must have been repeating itself all over the factory. GAX had weathered his transition, and was back up to full power. On his suit radio, Sta-Hi could hear the twittering bopper speech fading and dying out. Without the Happy Cloak he could no longer understand what they were saying.

Sta-Hi let himself fall to the ground, too, playing possum. The funny thing was that the robot remotes seemed relatively unaffected by the intense magnetic fields. To be able to move around in realtime, they must have some processors independent of BEX's big brain. But these small satellite brains wouldn't be complex enough to need the superconducting Josephson junctions of a full bopper brain.

Sta-Hi lay motionless, afraid to breathe. There was a long pause. Then, glass eyes blank, the remote picked up the electromagnet and lugged it off, looking for more intruders. Sta-Hi lay there another minute, wondering what kind of mind lay inside the shielded walls of the three-meter metal cube beside him. He decided to find out.

After glancing around to make sure the coast was clear of remotes, Sta-Hi crawled over and checked that the two wires were pushed well into the explosive putty he'd wedged under the base of the processor. He picked up the two spools of wire and the trigger-cell, and backed twenty meters off from the unit, paying out the wires as he went.

Then he squatted behind a stamping mill, poised his thumb over the button on the trigger-cell, and waited.

It was only a few minutes till one of the remotes spotted him. It ran towards him, carrying a heavy wrench.

"That's not going to work, GAX," Sta-Hi called. With the Cloak off he had his old voice back. He only hoped the big bopper spoke English. "One step closer and I push the button."

The remote stopped, three meters off. It looked like it might be about to throw the wrench. "Back off!" Sta-Hi cried, his voice cracking. "Back off or I'll push on three!" Did GAX understand?

"One!" The robot, lurching like a mechanical man, moved uncertainly.

"Two!" Sta-Hi began pushing the button, taking up the slack.

"Th-" Krypto the Killer Robot turned and walked off. And GAX began to talk.

"Don't be hasty, Mr. . . . *DeMentis*. Or do you prefer your *real* name?" The voice in his earphones was urbane and intimate, the mad mastermind taunting the trapped superhero.

Chapter Fifteen

Sta-Hi didn't answer right away. The dark mechanical-man remote stopped some ten meters off and turned to stare at him. He could hear his breathing more distinctly than usual. Muzak seemed to be playing faintly in the deep background somewhere. All over the factory, dark remotes had come out of hiding and were straightening up . . . dismantling the dead boppers and remotes, lining the work-tools back up, soldering loose wires back in place.

"You're not leaving here alive," GAX's voice said smoothly. "Not in your present form."

"Fuck that," Sta-Hi exclaimed. "I push this button and you're gone. *I'm* the one in charge here."

A high-pitched synthetic chuckle. "Yes . . . but my remotes are programmable for up to four days of independent activity. On their own they lack a certain intelligence . . . spirituality if you will. But they obey. I suggest that you reassess your situation."

Sta-Hi realized then that there was a loose ring of perhaps fifty remotes around him. All were seemingly at work, but all were acutely aware of his presence. He was hopelessly outnumbered.

"You see," Gax gloated. "We enjoy a situation of mutual assured destruction. Game-theoretically interesting, but by no means unprecedented. Your move." The ring of robots around Sta-Hi tightened a bit . . . a step here, a turn there . . . *something was crawling towards the wires!*

"Freeze!" Sta-Hi screamed, gripping the trigger-cell. "Anything else in here moves and I'm blowing the whole goddamn . . ."

Abruptly the factory fell silent. There were no more sidling movements, no more vibrations except for a deep, steady grinding somewhere underfoot. Sta-Hi finished screaming. There was a little blue light blinking on his wrist. Air warning. He checked the reading. Two hours left. He was going to have to stop breathing so hard.

"You should have gone with Ralph Numbers and Dr. Anderson," GAX said quietly. "To join the ranks of the immortal. As it is, you may become damaged too badly for effective taping."

"Why, GAX? Why do you cut people up and tape their brains?" Surges of mortal fear kept gripping Sta-Hi's guts. Why weren't there any pills inside the suit? He sucked greedily at the drinking nipple by his right cheek.

"We value information, Sta-Hi. Nothing is so densely packed with logically deep information as a human brain. This is the primary reason. MEX compares our activities to those American industrialists called . . . *culture-vultures*. Who ransacked the museums of the Old World for works of art. And there are higher, more spiritual reasons. The merging of all . . ."

"Why can't you just use EEG's?" Sta-Hi asked. The grinding vibration underfoot was getting stronger. A trap? He moved back a few meters. "Why do you have to *chew up* our brains?"

"So much of your information storage is chemical or mechanical rather than electrical," GAX explained. "A careful electron-microscopic mapping of the memory RNA strands is necessary. And by cutting the brain into thin slices we can learn which neurons connect to which. But this has gone on long enough, Sta-Hi. Drop the trigger-cell and we will tape you. Join us. You can be our third Earth-based robot-bodied agent. You'll see that . . ."

"You're not getting me," Sta-Hi interrupted. He was standing now and his voice had risen. "Soul-snatchers! Puppet-masters! I'd rather die clean, you goddamn . . ."

KKKKAA-BRRUUUUUUUUMMM

Without quite meaning to, Sta-Hi had pushed the button on the trigger-cell. The flash of light was blinding. Pieces of things flew past on hard, flat trajectories. There was no air to carry a shockwave, but the ground underfoot jerked and knocked him off his feet. Clumsy again, but numerous, the pre-programmed remotes moved in for the kill.

The whole time he had been talking with GAX there had been that steady grinding vibration coming through the floor. Now, as Sta-Hi stood up again, the vibration broke into a chunky mutter and something burst through the floor behind him. A blue and silver nose-cone studded with black drill-bits . . . a digger!

It twittered something oily. A wrench flew by. The remotes were closing in. Without a second thought, Sta-Hi followed the digger back down the tunnel it had made, crawling on his stomach like a shiny white worm.

It's a bad feeling not to be able to see your feet when you're expecting steel claws to sink into them. Sta-Hi crawled very fast. Before long, the thin tube they were in punched through the wall of a big tunnel, and Sta-Hi followed the digger out.

He got to his feet and brushed himself off. No punctures in his suit. An hour's worth of air left. He was going to have to stop getting excited and breathing so hard.

The digger was examining Sta-Hi curiously . . . circling him, and reaching out to touch him with a thin and flexible probe.

A small rock came rolling out of the shaft they had come down. The killer-robots were coming. "Uuuuunnh!" Sta-Hi said, pointing.

"To be rresstfulll," the digger said. He humped himself up like the numeral "2" and applied his digging head to the tunnel wall near the hole they'd crawled out of. Sta-Hi stepped back. Moments later a few tons of rock came loose, burying the digger and the hole he'd made.

A moment later the digger slid effortlessly out of the heap of rubble, leaving no exit behind him. "To

commme withh mme," he said, wriggling past Sta-Hi.
"I willl showw you thinngs of innteresst."

Sta-Hi followed along. Once again he was breathing
hard. "Do you have any air?" he asked.

"Whatt iss airr?"

Sta-Hi controlled his voice with difficulty. "It's a
. . . gas. With oxygen. Humans breathe it."

Sta-Hi's radio warbled strangely in his ear. Laughter?
"Of courrsse. *Aairr*. There iss plennty in the pinnk-
houses. Do yyou needd aairr in the presennt tensse?"

"In half an hour." The tunnel was unlit, and Sta-Hi
had to guide himself by following the blue-white glow of
the digger's body. Not too far ahead was a spot of pink-
ish light in the side of the tunnel.

"To be resstfull. In hallf a kilometerr iss a pinkk-
housse with nno nurrsies. But llook innto thiss one
firrsstt." The digger stopped by a pink-lit window.

Sta-Hi peered in. Ralph Numbers was in there with a
portable refrigeration unit plugged into his side. Warm in
there. Ralph was standing over a thing like a floppy
bathtub, and in it . . .

"Doctorr Annderssonn iss inn the nurssie," the digger
said softly.

The nursie was a big moist pod shaped something like
a soldier's cap, but two meters long. A big cunt-cap,
with six articulated metal arms on each side. The arms
were busy . . . horribly busy.

They had already flayed Cobb's torso. His chest was
split down the sternum. Two arms held the ribcage open,
while two others extracted the heart, and then the lungs.
At the same time, Ralph Numbers was easing Cobb's
brain out of the top of the opened-up skull. He discon-
nected the EEG wires from the brain, and then dropped
the brain into something that looked like a bread-slicer
connected to an X-ray machine.

The nursie flicked the switch on the brain-analyzer and
waddled away from the window, towards the far end of
the room.

"Nnow to pllannt," the digger whispered.

At the other end of the pink-lit room was a large tank
of murky fluid. The nursie moved down the tank, sow-

ing. Lungs here, kidneys there . . . squares of skin, eyeballs, testicles . . . each part of Cobb's body found its
place in the organ tank. Except for the heart. After examining the second-hand heart critically, the nursie threw
it down a disposal chute.

"What about the brain?" Sta-Hi whispered. He strug-
gled to understand. Cobb feared death above all else.
And the old man had *known* what he was in for here.
But he had chosen it anyhow. Why?

"The brainn patterns will be annalyzzed. Doctorr
Annderssonn's ssoftwarre will alll be preserrrved,
but . . ."

"But what?"

"Ssome of uss feel thiss is nnott rright. Especially in
those much morre frequennt cases where nno nnew
harrdware iss issuedd to the donorr. The bigg bopperrss
wannt to do thiss to alll the flesherrs and all the little
bopperrs, too. They wannt to mellt us all togetherr. We
arre fightinng backk, annd you havve hellped uss verry
much by killinng GAX."

Inside the room the nursie had finished. On its short
legs it waddled back to Ralph Numbers, standing there
with misery written all over his flicker-cladding. The
nursie came up next to Ralph, as if to say something.
But then, with a motion too fast to follow, it sprang up
and plastered itself to Ralph's body-box.

The red robot's manipulators struggled briefly and then
were still. "Yyou ssee!" the digger hissed. "Nnow it
iss stealinng Rallph's soffware too! No onne iss safe.
The warr musst conntinue till all the biggg bopperrs
havve . . ."

A thickness was growing in Sta-Hi's throat. Nausea?
He turned away from the window, took a step and stumbled to his knees. The blue light on his wrist glared in
his eyes. He was suffocating!

"Air," Sta-Hi gasped. The digger lifted him onto its
back and wriggled furiously down the tunnel to a safe
pink-house, an air-filled room with nothing but some un-
attended organ-tanks.

Chapter Sixteen

Strangely enough, Cobb never had the feeling of really losing consciousness. He and Ralph hurried through the tunnels to the pink-house together. In the pink-house, Ralph helped Cobb into the nursie, the nursie gave him a shot, and then everything . . . came loose.

There were suddenly so many possibilities for motion that Cobb was scared to move. He felt as if his legs might walk off in one direction and leave his head and arms behind.

But that wasn't quite accurate. For he couldn't really say where his arms or legs or head were. Maybe they had already walked off from each other and were now walking back. Or maybe they were doing both. With an effort he located what seemed to be one of his hands. But was it a right hand or a left hand? It was like asking if a coin in your pocket is heads or tails.

This sort of problem, however, was only a small part of Cobb's confusion, only the tip of the iceberg, the edge of the wedge, the snout of the camel, the first crocus of spring, the last rose of summer, the ant and the grasshopper, the little engine that could, the third sailor in the whorehouse, the Cthulhu Mythos, the neural net, two scoops of green ice-cream, a broken pane of glass, Borges's essay on time, the year 1982, the state of Florida, Turing's imitation game, a stuffed platypus, the smell of Annie Cushing's body, an age-spot shaped like Australia, the cool moistness of an evening in March, the Bell inequality, the taste of candied violets, a chest-pain like a steel cylinder, Aquinas's definition of God, the smell of black ink, two lovers seen out a window, the clack of typing, the white moons on fingernails, the world as construct, rotten fishbait on a wooden dock, the fear of the self that fears, aloneness, maybe, yes and no . . .

"Cobb?"

If he answered then he must not have. That is, if he hadn't answered, he would have. To say: *Help me, Ralph!* To say: *Whoooooooooooooooooah!!* To say: *Here come de judge!!!* To say: *Selection principles must occur at every level of the processor hierarchy.* To say: *Please don't.* To say: *Verena.* To say: *Possibility is Reality!* To say: DzzzZZzZZZZzZZZZZzzzZzZZZZzzzzZZzZz ZZZZZzzzzZzZZzZZZZzzzZZZzZZZZzzt. To say the noise and information all at once; Lord, just this once . . .

"Cobb?"

The confusion was thicker now, distinctions gone. He had always thought that thought processes depended on picking points on a series of yes-or-no scales . . . but now the scales were gone, or bent into circles, and he was still thinking. Amazing what a fellow can do without. Without past or future, black or white, right or left, fat or thin, pokes or strokes . . . *they're all the same* . . . me or you, space or time, finite or infinite, being or nothingness . . . *make it real* . . . Christmas or Easter, acorns or oak trees, Annie or Verena, flags or toilet-paper, looking at clouds or hearing the sea, ham-spread or tuna, asses or tits, fathers or sons . . .

"Cobb?"

Chapter Seventeen

It happened while he was buying an ice-cream, a double-size Mr. Frostee with sprinkles. The driver counted the change into Cobb's hand and suddenly he was . . . there again. But where had he been?

Cobb started, and stared at the truck-driver, an evil-looking bald man with half his teeth missing. Something like a wink or a smile seemed to flicker across the ruined face. Then the sickly sweet chiming started up again and the boxy white truck drove off, its powerful refrigeration unit humming away.

His feet carried him back to his beach cottage. Annie was on the porch in back, lounging on Cobb's hammock with her shirt off. She was rubbing baby oil into the soft rolls of her belly-flesh.

"Give me a lick, honey?"

Cobb looked at her, uncomprehending. Since when was *she* living with him? But . . . yet . . . he could remember her moving in with him last Friday night. Today was Friday again. She'd been here a week. He could remember the week, but it was like remembering a book or a movie . . .

"Come on, Cobb, before it melts!"

Annie leaned out from the hammock, her brown breasts sliding around. He handed her the ice-cream cone. *Ice-cream cone?*

"I don't like ice-cream," Cobb said. "You can have it all."

Annie sucked at the cold tip, her full lips rounded. Coyly, she glanced over to see if Cobb was thinking what she was. He wasn't.

"Whydja buy it then?" she asked with a slight edge to her voice. "When you heard that music you went running out of here like you'd been waiting your whole life to hear it. First time I've seen you excited all week." There was a hint of accusation in the last sentence, of disappointment.

"All week," Cobb echoed and sat down. It was funny how supple his body felt. He didn't have to keep his back stiff. He held his hands up, flexing them curiously. He felt so strong.

Of course he had to be strong, to break out of his crate and through the warehouse wall, with only Sta-Hi to help him . . . *What?*

The memories were all there, the sights and sounds, but something was missing from them. Something he suddenly had again.

"I am," Cobb muttered. "I am me." He . . . this body . . . hadn't thought that for . . . how long?

"That's good, hon." Annie was lying back in the hammock, her hands folded over her navel. "You've been acting kind of weird ever since Mooney took us to the Gray Area last Friday. *I am. I am me.* That's all there is really, isn't there. . . ." She kicked out with her bare foot, setting the hammock to swaying.

The operation must have worked. It was all fitting together now. The frantic dash to the pink-house with Ralph. The nursie, the shot, and then that strange floating time of total disorientation.

Under these memories, faint but visible, were the robot's memories: Breaking out of the warehouse, contacting the old Anderson on the beach, and then moving in with Annie. That had been last week, last Friday.

Since then that cop, Mooney, had been out twice more to talk to him. But he hadn't realized the real Cobb was gone. The robot had been able to fake it by just acting too drunk to answer specific questions. Even though Mooney had begun to suspect that Cobb had a robot double somewhere, he was naive enough to think he'd know the double on sight.

"There's Sta-Hi," Annie called. "Will you let him in, Cobb?"

"Sure." He stood up easily. Sta-Hi always dropped by this time of day. Nights he guarded a warehouse at the spaceport. They liked to fish together. *They did?*

Cobb walked into the kitchen and peered through the screen door, holding the handle uncertainly. That sure looked like Sta-Hi out there in the harsh sun, skinny and shirtless, his lips stretched in a half-smile.

"Hi," Cobb said, as he had said every day for a week. "How are you?"

"Stuzzy," Sta-Hi said, smiling and tossing his hair back. "Waving." He reached for the door handle.

But Cobb continued to hold the door closed. "Hi," he said, on a wild impulse. "How are you?"

"Stuzzy," Sta-Hi said, smiling and tossing his hair back. "Waving." He reached for the door handle.

"Hi," Cobb said, trying to keep the tremble out of his voice. "How are you?"

"Stuzzy," Sta-Hi said, smiling and tossing his hair back. "Waving." He reached for the door handle.

Music was playing, wheedling closer. Resonant as a film of mucus across a public-speaker's throat . . . har-rumph . . . sweet as a toothache, it's Mister Frostee time!

Sta-Hi jerked and turned around. He was hurrying to-wards the white truck that was slowly cruising up.

"*More* ice-cream?" Annie asked as Cobb opened the door to follow.

The door slapped shut. Annie kicked again, swaying gently. Today she wouldn't cover up her breasts when Sta-Hi came in. Her nipples were a definite plus. She poured out a bit more baby oil. *One* of them was going to take her to the Golden Prom tonight and that was that.

Cobb followed the Sta-Hi thing . . . Sta-Hi$_2$ . . . out to the Mr. Frostee truck. The sun was very bright. The same bald man with the half-caved-in face was driving. What a guy to have selling ice-cream. He looked like a thrill-killer.

The driver stopped when he saw Sta-Hi$_2$, and gave him a familiar smile. At least it might have been a smile. Sta-Hi$_2$ walked up to him expectantly.

"A double-dip Mr. Frostee with sprinkles on it."

"Yeth *thir!*" the driver said, his loose lips fluttering. He got out and unlatched the heavy door in the truck's side. He wore colorful sneakers with letters around the edges. Kid's shoes, but big.

"Thtick your head in," the driver advised, "an you'll *get* it!"

Cobb tried to see over Sta-Hi$_2$'s shoulder. There was much too much equipment in that truck. And it was *so cold* in there. Frost crystals formed in the air that blew out. In the middle was what looked like a giant vacuum chamber, even colder, shrouded and insulated. A double-dip Mr. Frostee with sprinkles was sitting there in a sort of bracket set one meter back. Had it been that way for Cobb? He couldn't remember.

It didn't seem to bother the driver that Cobb was watching. They were all in this together. Sta-Hi$_2$ leaned in, reaching for that cone.

There was a flash of light, four flashes, one from each corner of the door. The skinny arm snagged the cone, and the figure turned around utterly expressionless.

"Yes no no no yes no no no yes yes yes no no no yes no no yes yes yes no yes yes yes yes no no . . ." it muttered, dropping the cone. It turned and shuffled towards Cobb's house. The feet stayed on the ground at all times, and left two plowed-up grooves in the crushed shell driveway. ". . . no yes no no no."

The driver looked upset. "Whath with him? Heth thuppothed to . . ."

He hurried into the truck's cab and talked for a minute over what seemed to be a CB radio. Then he came back out, looking relieved.

"I didn't wealize. Mithter Fwostee jutht bwoke contact with him. The weal Thta-Hi ith coming back . . . he got away. Tho the wemote'll need a new cover. Jutht lay him on your bed for now. We'll pick him up tonight."

The half-faced driver jumped back into the truck and drove off with a cheery wave. Somehow he had brought Cobb back to life, but he had turned Sta-Hi off instead. They hadn't had a brain-tape to put into the robot. And with the real Sta-Hi coming back intact they'd decided to turn it off.

Cobb took the Sta-Hi thing's arm, trying to help it towards his house. The features on the tortured face were distorted almost beyond recognition. The mouth worked, tongue humping up like an epileptic's.

"Yes no no yes yes yes no no no no yes yes . . ."

Machine language. It raised one of its clawed hands, trying to block the bright sunlight.

Cobb led it to the front steps, and it stumbled heavily. It didn't seem to have the concept of lifting its feet. He held the door open, and the Sta-Hi thing came in on all fours, hands and knees shuffling along.

"What's the matter?" Annie asked, coming into the kitchen from the back porch. "Is he tripping?" She was in the mood for some excitement. It would be really neat to show up stoned at the Prom. "You got any more, Sta-Hi?"

The anguished figure fell over onto its side now, thick tongue protruding, lips drawn back in rictus death-grin. Its arms were wrapped around its chest, and the legs were frantically bicycling up some steep and heartless grade. The leg-motions slowly pulled the body around and around in circles on the kitchen floor.

Annie backed off, changing her mind about taking this trip.

"Cobb! He's having a fit!"

Cobb could almost understand it now. There was some machinery in that Mr. Frostee truck, machinery which had brought his own consciousness back to him. Machinery which had done something else to Sta-Hi$_2$. Turned it off.

The twitching on the floor damped down, oscillation by oscillation. Then the Sta-Hi thing was still, utterly still.

"Call a doctor, Cobb!"

Annie was all the way back on the porch, peering into the kitchen with both hands over her mouth.

''A doctor can't help him, Annie. I don't think he was even . . .'' He couldn't say it.

Cobb bent over and picked the limp form up as easily as a rag-doll. Amazing the strength they'd built in. He carried the body down the short hall and laid it on his bed.

Chapter Eighteen

Mooney lit a cigarette and stepped into the patch of shade under the space-shuttle's stubby wing. Starting with this shipment, every crate shipped from Disky had to be opened and inspected, right out here on the goddamn field. The superheated air hanging over the expanse of concrete shimmered in the afternoon sun. Not a ghost of a breeze.

"Here's the last bunch, Mr. Mooney." Tommy looked down at him from the hatch. Six tight plastic containers glided down on the power-lift. "Interferon and a couple of crates of organs."

Mooney turned and gave a high-sign to the platoon of armed men standing in the sun fifteen meters off. Almost quitting time. Still puffing his cigarette, he turned back to eye the last set of crates. It was going to be a bitch getting those things open.

"Who was the asshole who had the bright idea of searching crates for stowaway robots?" Tommy asked, sliding down the lift.

A rivulet of sweat ran into Mooney's eye. Slowly he drew out his handkerchief and mopped his face again. "Me," he said. "I'm the asshole. There's been two break-ins at Warehouse Three. At least we thought they were break-ins. Both times there were some empty crates and a hole in the wall. Routine organ theft, right? Well . . . the second time I noticed that the debris from the holes was on the outside of the building. I figure what we had here was a break-*out*. The boppers have snuck at least three robots down on us, the way I see it."

Tommy looked dubious. "Has anyone ever *seen* one of these robots?"

"I almost had one of them myself. But I didn't realize it till it was too late." Mooney had been back at Cobb's twice . . . hoping to find the old man's robot double. But there had just been the old man there, drunk as usual. No way to know where the robot was now . . . hell, it could probably even change its face. *If* it even existed. He'd searched almost this whole shipment now, and still hadn't found anything.

Mooney ground out his cigarette. "It could be I'm wrong, though." He stepped into the sun and began examining the fastenings on the next crate. "I *hope* I'm wrong."

What, after all, did he really have to go on? Just some scraps of wall-board lying outside the warehouse instead of inside. And a faint glimpse of a running figure that had reminded him of old Cobb Anderson. And seeing a guy who had looked like Cobb's twin at the Gray Area last week. But he hoped he was wrong, and that nothing bad would happen, now that his life was settling into a comfortable groove.

Young Stanny was living at home again. That was the main thing. His narrow escape from those brain-eaters seemed to have sobered him. Ever since the police had brought him back he'd been a model son. And with Stanny back in the house, Bea had straightened out a little, too.

Mooney had gotten his son a job as a night watchman at the spaceport . . . and the kid was taking his work seriously! He hadn't fucked-up yet! At this rate he'd be handling the whole watch-system for the warehouses inside of six months.

Daytimes Stanny wasn't home much. Incredible how little sleep that boy needed. He'd catch a catnap after work and then he'd be off for the day. Mooney worried a little about what Stanny might be up to all day, but it couldn't be too bad. Whatever it was it couldn't be too bad.

Every evening, regular as clockwork, Stanny would show up for supper, usually a little tranked-out, but never roaring stoned like he used to get. It was just amazing how he'd straightened out ever . . .

"I've cracked the seal," Tommy repeated.

Mooney's attention snapped back to the task at hand. Six more crates and they'd be through for the day. This one was supposed to be full of interferon ampules. The gene-spliced bacteria that produced the anti-cancer drug grew best in the sterile, low-temperature lunar environment. Mooney helped Tommy lift the lid off, and they peered in.

No problem. It was full of individual vacuum-sealed syringes, loaded and ready to go. Halfheartedly, Mooney dug down into the crate, making sure that nothing else was in there. Passed. Tommy switched on the conveyor-belt, and the crate glided across the field, past the armed men, and into Warehouse Three.

The next three crates were the same. But the last two . . . there was something funny about the last two. For one thing they were stuck together to make a double-size crate. And the label read "HUMAN ORGANS: MIXED." Usually a crate was all livers or all kidneys . . . always all one thing. He'd never seen a mixed crate yet.

The box was vacuum-tight, and it took a few minutes work with the pry-bars to break the seals. Mooney wondered what would be in there . . . a Whitman's sampler assortment? Glazed eyeballs on paper doilies, a big liver like a brazil-nut, crunchy marrow-filled femurs, a row of bean-shaped kidneys, a king-size penis coyly curled against its testicles, chewy ropes of muscles, big squares of skin rolled up like apricot leather?

The lid splintered suddenly. *Something was coming out!*

Mooney sprang back, screaming a "*READY!*" to the soldiers. Their weapons were instantly at their shoulders.

The whole lid flew off now, and a shining silvery head poked out. A figure stood up, humanoid, glittering silver in the sun. Tubes connected it to further machinery in the box . . .

"*AIM!*" Mooney cried, backing well out of the line of fire.

The silver figure seemed to hear him, and began tearing at its head. A detachable bomb? Tommy cut and run, straight towards the troops. The fool! He was right in the line of fire! Mooney backed off, glancing desperately back and forth, waiting to give the *FIRE* command.

Suddenly the bubble-top came off the silvery figure's suit. There was a face underneath, the face of . . .

"Wait, Dad! It's me!"

Sta-Hi tore the air-hoses loose and tried to jump behind the box before anyone could shoot. His legs were cramped from thirty hours in the crates. He moved awkwardly. His foot caught on the edge of the crate, and he sprawled onto the concrete apron.

Mooney ran forward, putting his body between the crate and the troops.

"AT EASE!" he hollered, leaning over his son. But if this was his son . . . who had been living at his house all week?

"Is it really you, Stanny? How did you get in the box?"

Sta-Hi just lay there for a minute, grinning and stroking the rough concrete. "I've been to the Moon. And call me *Sta-Hi,* dammit, how many times do I have to tell you?"

Chapter Nineteen

Cobb spent the afternoon trying to get drunk. Somehow Annie had gotten him to promise they'd go to the Golden Prom together, but he was damned if he wanted to be anything other than blacked-out by the time he got there.

It was funny the way she had convinced him. They'd closed the door on . . . on Sta-Hi$_2$ . . . and gone out to the porch together. And then, sitting there looking at Annie, wondering what to say, it was as if Cobb had fallen through her eyes, into her mind, feeling her body sensations even, and her desperate longing for a bit more fun, a little gaiety at the end of what had been a long, hard life. Before she'd even said a word he'd been convinced.

And now she was dressing or washing her hair or something and he was sitting on the stretch of beach behind his little pink cottage. Annie had stocked his cupboard with sherry earlier this week, hoping to get some kind of rise out of him, but, except when Mooney had come snooping around, it had sat there untouched, along with the food. Thinking back, he couldn't recall this new body of his having drunk or eaten much of anything during the last week. Of course he'd had to chew down some of the fish he and Sta-Hi$_2$ had caught. Annie always insisted on frying it up for them. And when old Mooney had come, he'd sipped some sherry and pretended to be drunk. But other than that . . .

Cobb opened a second bottle of sherry and pulled deeply at it. The first bottle had done nothing but make him belch a few times, incredibly foul-smelling belches, methane and hydrogen-sulfide, death and corruption going on somewhere deep inside him. His mind was clear as a bell, and he was tired of it.

Suddenly exasperated, Cobb tilted up the second bottle of sherry, and, leaving an airspace above his upper lip, chugged the whole fucking thing down in one long, drink-crazed gurgle.

As he swallowed the last of it he felt a sudden and acute distress. But it wasn't the buzz, the flush, the confusion he had expected. It was, rather, an incredible urgency, a need to . . .

Without even consciously controlling what he did, Cobb knelt down on the sand and clawed at the vertical scar on his chest. *He was too full.* Finally he pushed the right spot and the little door in his chest popped open. He tried not to breathe as the rotten fish and lukewarm sherry plopped down onto the sand in front of him. Yyeeeeeeaaaaauuughhhh.

He stood up, still moving automatically, and went inside to rinse the food cavity out with water. And it wasn't till he was wiping it out with paper towels that he thought to notice anything strange about what he was doing.

He stopped then, a wad of paper towels in his hand, and stared down. The little door was metal on the inside and plastic flicker-cladding on the out. After he pushed it shut the skin dove-tailed so well that he couldn't find the top edge. He found the pressure switch again . . . just under his left nipple . . . and popped the little door back open. There were scratches on the metal . . . writing? It looked backwards, but he couldn't bend close enough to be sure.

Door flapping, Cobb went into the bathroom and examined himself in the mirror. Except for the hole in his chest he looked the same as ever. He *felt* the same as ever. But now he was a robot.

He pushed the little door all the way open, so that the metal inside was reflected in the mirror. There was a letter there, scratched in backwards.

Dear Dr. Anderson!

Welcome to your new hardware! Use it in good repair as a token of gratitude from the entire bopper race!

User's Guide:

1) Your body's skeleton, muscles, processors, etc. are synthetic and self-repairing. Be sure, however, to re-charge the power-cells twice a year. Plug is located in left heel.

2) Your brain-functions are partially contained in a remote super-cooled processor. Avoid electromagnetic shielding or noise-sources, as this may degrade the body-brain link. Travel should be undertaken only after con-sultation.

3) Every effort has been made to transfer your soft-ware without distortion. In addition we have built in a library of useful subroutines. Access under password BE-BOPALULA.

Respectfully yours,

The Big Boppers

Cobb sat down on the toilet and locked the bathroom door. Then he got up and read the letter again. It was still sinking in. Intellectually he had always known it was possible. A robot, or a person, has two parts: hardware and software. The hardware is the actual physical ma-terial involved, and the software is the pattern in which the material is arranged. Your *brain* is hardware, but the *information* in the brain is software. The mind . . . memories, habits, opinions, skills . . . is all software. The boppers had extracted Cobb's software and put it in control of this robot body. Everything was working per-fectly, according to plan. For some reason this made Cobb angry.

"Immortality, my ass," he said, kicking the bathroom door. His foot went through it.

"Goddamn stupid robot leg."

He unlocked the door and walked down the hall into the kitchen. Christ, he needed a drink. The thing that bothered Cobb the most was that even though he *felt* like he was all here, his brain was *really* inside a computer somewhere else. Where?

Suddenly he knew. The Mr. Frostee truck, of course. A super-cooled bopper brain was in that truck, with Cobb's software all coded up. It could simulate Cobb Anderson to perfection, and it monitored and controlled the robot's actions at the speed of light.

Cobb thought back to that interim time, before the simulation that was now him had hooked into a new body. There had been no distinctions, no nagging facts, only raw possibility . . . Thinking back to the experience opened up his consciousness in a strange way. As if he could let himself go and ooze out into the rooms and houses around him. For an instant he saw Annie's face staring out of a mirror, tweezers and tube of cream . . .

He was standing in front of the kitchen sink. He'd left the water running. He leaned forward and splashed some of it on his face. Something bumped the sink, oh yes, the door in his chest, and he pushed it closed. What had been that code word?

Cobb went back to the bathroom, opened the flap, and read the letter a third time. This time he got the little joke. The big boppers had put him in this body, and the code word for the library of subroutines was, of course,

"Be-Bop-A-Lu-La, she's mah baybee," Cobb sang, his voice echoing off the tiles, "Be-Bop-A-Lu-La, Ah don't mean maybee . . ." He stopped then, cocking his head to listen to an inner voice.

"Library accessed," it said.

"List present subroutines," Cobb commanded.

"MISTER FROSTEE, TIME-LINE, ATLAS, CALCULATOR, SENSE ACUITY, SELF-DESTRUCT, REFERENCE LIBRARY, FACT-CHUNKING, SEX, HYPERACTIVITY, DRUNKENNESS . . ."

"Hold it," Cobb cried. "Hold it right there. What does DRUNKENNESS involve?"

"Do you wish to call the subroutine?"

"First tell me what it does." Cobb opened the bathroom door and glanced out nervously. He thought he had heard something. It wouldn't do for him to be found talking to himself. If people suspected he was a robot they might lynch . . .

". . . now activated," the voice in his head was saying in its calm, know-it-all tone. "Your senses and thought processes will be systematically distorted in a step-wise fashion. Close your right nostril and breathe in once through your *left* nostril for each step desired. Inhaling repeatedly through the *right* nostril will reverse these steps. There is, of course, an automatic override for your . . ."

"O.K.," Cobb said. "Now stop talking. Log off. End it."

"The command you are searching for is OUT, Dr. Anderson."

"OUT, then."

The feeling of another presence in his mind winked out. He walked out onto the back porch and stared at the ocean for awhile. The bad smell from the rotten fish drifted in. Cobb found a piece of cardboard and took it out to scoop the mess up. *Re-charge power-cells twice a year.*

He dumped the stinking fish down by the water's edge and walked back to his cottage. Something was bothering him. How likely was it that this new body was a *token of gratitude* with no strings attached?

Obviously the body had been sent to Earth with certain built-in programs . . . break out of the warehouse, tell Cobb Anderson to go to the Moon, stick your head in the first Mr. Frostee truck you see. The big question was: were there any more programs waiting to be carried out? Worse: were the boppers in a position to control him on a real-time basis? Would he notice the difference? Who, in short, was in charge now, Cobb . . . or a big bopper called Mr. Frostee?

His mind felt clear as a bell, clear as a goddamn bell. Suddenly he remembered the other robot. Cobb went in through the porch and down the short hall to his bedroom. The bopper-built body that had looked like Sta-Hi was still lying there. Its features had gone slack and sagging. Cobb leaned over the body, listening. Not a sound. This one was turned off.

Why? "The real Sta-Hi is coming back," the truckdriver had said. So they wanted to get this one out of circulation before it was exposed as a robot. It had been standing in for Sta-Hi, working with Mooney at the spaceport. The plan had been for the robot to smuggle a whole lot more robot-remotes through customs and out of the warehouses. It had mentioned this to Cobb one day while they were fishing. Why so many robots?

Tokens of gratitude, each and every one? No way. *What did the boppers want?*

He heard the screen-door slap then. It was Annie. She'd done something to her hair and face. Seeing him, she shone like a sunflower.

"It's almost six, Cobb. I thought maybe we should walk over to the Gray Area now and have some supper there first?" He could feel her fragile happiness as clearly as if it were his own. He walked over and kissed her.

"You look beautiful." She had on a loose Hawaiian-print dress.

"But you, Cobb, you should change your clothes!"

"Right."

She followed him into his bedroom and helped him find the white-duck pants and the black sport-shirt she'd gotten ready for tonight.

"What about him?" Annie asked, whispering and pointing at the inert figure on Cobb's bed.

"Let him sleep. Maybe he'll pull through." The truck would come get him while they were out. Good riddance.

He could see through her eyes as he dressed. His new body wasn't quite as fat as the old one, and the clothes fit, for once, without stretching.

"I was afraid you'd be drunk," Annie said hesitantly.

"I *could* use a quick one," Cobb said. His new sensitivity to other people's thoughts and feelings was almost too much to take. "Wait a second."

Presumably the DRUNKENNESS subroutine was still activated. Cobb went into the kitchen, pressed his finger to his right nostril, and inhaled deeply. A warm feeling of relaxation hit him in the pit of the stomach and the backs of the knees, spreading out from there. It felt like a double shot of bourbon.

"That's better," Cobb murmured. He opened and closed the kitchen cupboard to sound as if he'd had a bottle out. Another quick snort, and then Annie came in. Cobb felt good.

"Let's go, baby. We'll paint the town red."

Chapter Twenty

"They're collecting human brain-tapes," Sta-Hi said as his father parked the car. "And sometimes they take apart the person's body, too, to seed their organ tanks. They've got a couple hundred brains on tap now. And at least three of those people have been replaced by robot doubles. There's Cobb, and one of the Little Kidders, and a stewardess. And there's still that robot who looks like me. Your surrogate son."

Mooney turned off the ignition and stared out across the shopping-center's empty parking lot. An unpleasant thought struck him.

"How do I know you're real *now*, Stanny? How do I know you're not another machine like the one that had me fooled all week?"

The answering laugh was soft and bitter. "You don't. *I* don't. Maybe the diggers switched me over while I was sleeping." Sta-Hi savored the worry on his father's face. *My son the cyborg.* Then he relented.

"You don't have to worry, Dad. The diggers wouldn't really do that. It's just the big boppers that are into it. The diggers only work there, making the tunnels. They're on our side, really. They've started a full-scale revolution on the Moon. Who knows, in a month there may be no big boppers left at all."

A dog ran across the parking lot, keeping an eye on their car. They could hear loud rock music from two blocks away. The pheezers were having some kind of party at the Gray Area bar tonight. In the distance the surf beat, and a cooling night breeze flickered in and out of the car windows.

"Well, Stanny . . ."

"Call me *Sta-Hi*, Dad. Which reminds me. You holding?"

Mooney rummaged in his glove compartment. There should be a pack of reefer in there somewhere . . . he'd confiscated it from one of his men who'd been smoking on duty . . . there it was.

"Here, Sta-Hi. Make yourself at home."

Sta-Hi pulled a face at the crumpled pack of cheap roach-weed, but lit up nonetheless. His first hit of anything since back at the Disky Hilton with that Misty girl. It had been a rough week hiding out in the pink-houses and then getting smuggled back to earth as a shipment of spare innards. Rough. He smoked down the first jay and lit another. The music outside focussed into note-for-note clarity.

"I bet old Anderson's at that party," Mooney said, rolling up his window. Damned if he was going to sit here while his son smoked a whole pack of dope. "Let's go check out his house, Sta-Hi."

"O.K." The dope was hitting Sta-Hi hard . . . he'd lost his tolerance. His legs were twitching and his teeth were chattering. A dark stain of death-fear spread across his mind. Carefully, he put the pack of reefers in his pocket. Must be good stuff after all.

Father and son walked across the parking lot, behind the stores and onto the beach. The moon, past full, angled its silvery light down onto the water. Crabs scuttled across their path and nipped into hidey-holes. It had been a long time since the two of them had walked together. Mooney had to hold himself back from putting an arm across his son's shoulders.

"I'm glad you're back," he said finally. "That robot copy of you . . . it always said yes. It was nice, but it wasn't you."

Sta-Hi flashed a quick smile, then patted his father on the back. "Thanks. I'm glad you're glad."

"Why . . ." Mooney's voice cracked and he started again. "Why can't you settle down now, Stanny? I could help you find a job. Don't you want to get married and . . ."

"And end up like you and Ma? No thanks." Too harsh. He tried again. "Sure I'd like to have a job, to do something important. But I don't *know* anything. I can't even learn how to play the guitar good. I'm only . . ." Sta-Hi spread his hands and laughed helplessly, "I'm only good at waving . . . at being cool. It's the only thing I've learned how to do in twenty-four years. What else can I do?"

"You . . ." Mooney fell silent, thinking. "Maybe you could make something out of this adventure you've had. Write a story or something. Hell, Stanny, you're *meant* to be a creative person. I don't want to see you end up wearing a badge like me. I could have been an illustrator, but I never made my move. You have to take that first step. No one can do it for you."

"I know that, too. But whenever I start something it's like I'm . . . a *nobody* who doesn't know *anything*. Mr. Nobody from Nowhere. And I can't process that. If I'm not going to win out anyway, I'd rather just . . ."

"You've got a good brain," Mooney told his son for what must have been the thousandth time. "You tested 92nd percentile on the MAGs and then you . . ."

"Yeah, yeah," Sta-Hi said, suddenly impatient. "Let's talk about something else. Like what are we going to do at Cobb's house anyway?" They had walked a couple of kilometers. The cottages couldn't be much further.

"You're *sure* they built robots to look like you and like Anderson?" Mooney asked.

"Right. But I don't know if the robots still look like us or not. They use this stuff called flicker-cladding for the skin, and it's full of little wires so if you pass different currents through it, the stuff looks different."

"But you figure Anderson's in one of these robots now?"

"Come shot! For sure. I saw a nursie taking him apart. It . . ." Sta-Hi broke off, laughing hard. Suddenly, with a reefer in him, the image of Cobb lying down in that giant toothed vagina . . . it was too funny for words. It was so good to be stoned again.

"But why lure you and him all the way up to the Moon just to tape your brain-patterns?"

"I don't know. Maybe they respect him too much to just kidnap him and eat his brain like anyone else. Or maybe they don't have any really *good* brain-dissecting machinery down here. And me . . . they just wanted to get me out of sight any way that . . ."

"Ssshhhh. We're there."

Thirty meters to their right was Cobb Anderson's cottage, silhouetted against the moon-bright sky. The light was bright enough to show the Mooneys up clearly, should anyone . . . anything . . . be looking. They doubled back to where a stand of palms reached down to near the water's edge and crept up to the cottages, staying in shadow.

The cottages were dark and deserted. It seemed like all the pheezers were out partying this Friday night. Mooney and Sta-Hi sidled along the cottage walls until they came to Cobb's. Mooney held them there, listening for a long two minutes. There was only the regular crash and hiss of the sea.

Sta-Hi followed his father in through the screen door and onto the porch. So this was where old Cobb had lived. Looked pleasant enough. Sta-Hi looked forward to being a pheezer himself someday . . . which only left about forty more years to waste.

Mooney put on a pair of goggles and flicked on his infra-red snooper light. He'd forgotten to bring it last Friday. He looked the room over. Lipsticked cigarette butts, baby oil, a wet bikini . . . *signs of female occupancy.*

That old white-haired babe was still living here. All week she'd been here with, Mooney now realized, Cobb's robot double. The two of them had been living here together waiting, though she didn't know it, for Cobb's mind to show up. Had it?

Briefly Mooney wondered if the robots could fuck. He could use a bionic cock himself, to keep Bea happy. If that whore hadn't always been sneaking out to the sex-clubs, Stanny never would have . . .

"What the fuck are you doing?" Sta-Hi demanded loudly. "Talking to yourself? I can't see a damn thing."

"Hussshhhhh. Put these on. I forgot." Mooney handed Sta-Hi the second pair of infra-light goggles.

The room cleared up for Sta-Hi then. The light was so red it looked blue. "Let's try the bedroom," he suggested.

"O.K."

Mooney led the way again. When he pushed open the bedroom door and shone his snooper light in, he had to bite his tongue to keep from screaming. Stanny was lying there, his features blurred and melted, the nose flopped over to one side and sagging down the cheek, the folded hands puddled like mittens.

Sta-Hi let out a low hissing noise and stepped forward, leaning over the inert robot on Cobb's bed. "Here's your perfect son, Dad. Be the first one on your block to see your boy come home in a box. The big boppers must have found out I was back. One of us had to go."

"But what's happened to it?" Mooney asked, approaching hesitantly. "It looks half-melted."

"It's a robot-remote. The central processor must have turned it off. There's a circuit in there for holding the flicker-cladding in shape, but . . ."

There was the sudden crunch of gravel, so close it seemed to be in the room with them. An engine was running, and a heavy door slammed. People were coming!

There was no time to run out through the house. Feet were already pounding up the front steps. Mooney grabbed his son and pulled him into Anderson's closet. There was no time to say anything to each other.

"Mr. Fwostee thaid he'th in the bedwoom, Buhdoo."

"Hey, Rainbow! Git yore skanky ass in here and help me lug this sucker out!"

"Ah don't see *wha* you big strong meyun cain't do it alone."

"I thtarted a hewnia yethterday wifting thomething."

"Liftin whut, Haf-N-Haf, yore pecker?"

The three voices shared a moment of laughter at this sally.

"*The Little Kidders,*" Sta-Hi breathed into his father's ear. Mooney elbowed him sharply for silence. A coathanger rattled, *oh shit,* but the voices were still out in the living-room.

"This's a naahce pad, ain't it, Berdoo?"

"Y'all want one lahk it, Rainbow honey? Stick with me an yore gonna be fartin through silk."

"Thass sweet, Berdoo."

"You two wovebihds bwing the body out, and I'll watch the twuck." Haf-N-Haf's heavy footsteps went back down the steps. The truck door slammed again.

Berdoo and Rainbow walked into the bedroom.

"Whah . . . isn't he a *saaht?* He looks lahk a devilfish!"

"Don't you worry yore purty haid. He'll taahten up onct Mr. Frostee reprograms him."

"But wait, hunneh. Don't he remaahnd yew of the man who's brain we almost ate that taam? Last week over to Kristleen's?"

"This ain't a *man,* Rainbow. This here's a switched-off *robot.* I don't know what the hail *man* you're talking about, girl."

"Ooooh nevvah mahnd. Ah'll git his laigs an you take tother eyund."

"Okey-doke. Watch yer step, the sucker's heavy."

Grunting a little, Berdoo and Rainbow wrestled the body out of Cobb's house and down the steps. The whole time, the truck's engine ran.

Cautiously, Mooney stuck his head out the closet door. The bedroom had a window on either side, and through one window he could make out the dark mass of an ice-cream truck. There was a big plastic cone on top of the cab.

Two dim figures stopped at the side of the truck and laid something heavy on the ground. A third man climbed down out of the cab, and opened a door in the side.

One of them turned on a light then, light which picked out every object in the bedroom. Terrified, Mooney threw himself back into the closet. He made Sta-Hi stay in there with him until they heard the truck drive off.

Chapter Twenty-one

Cobb chewed down his broiled fish with apparent relish, and managed to enjoy his wine by taking one DRUNKENNESS snort through his left nostril for every two glasses. After dinner he went to the men's room and emptied out his food unit . . . not because he had to, but just to reassure himself that it was really true.

He was feeling the effect now of a good five or six whiskeys, and the whole situation didn't seem so horrible and frightening as it initially had. Hell, he had it *made*. As long as he kept his batteries charged there was no reason he couldn't live another twenty years . . . scratch that, another *century!* It was only a question of how long the machine could hold up. And even that didn't matter . . . the big boppers had him taped and could project him onto as many bodies as he needed.

Cobb stood, swaying a bit, in front of the men's room mirror. *A fine figure of a man.* He looked the same as ever, white beard and all, but the eyes . . . He leaned closer, staring into his eyes. Something was a little off there, it was the irises, they were too uniform, not fibrous enough. Big deal. He was immortal! He took another jolt through his left nostril and went out to join Annie.

While they had been eating, the band had set up in the hall behind the Gray Area, and now enough pheezers had arrived for them to start playing. Annie took Cobb's hand and led him into the dance-hall. She had helped decorate it herself.

Overhead they had a big, slowly spinning ball covered with a mosaic of tiny square mirrors. From each corner of the room a colored spotlight shone on the ball, and the reflected flecks of light spun endlessly around the room, changing colors as they moved from wall to wall. There had been a mirror-ball exactly like this at Annie's Senior Prom in 1970, lo these fifty years gone.

"Do you like it, Cobb?"

It made Cobb a little dizzy. This subroutined DRUNKENNESS wasn't quite like the real thing. He held his finger to the left side of his nose and took two quick breaths through his right nostril, coming down a couple of notches, enough to enjoy himself again.

The lights were perfect, really, it made you feel like you were on a boatride down some sun-flecked creek, trout hovering just beneath the surface, and all the time in the world . . .

"It's beautiful, Annie. Just like being young again. Shall we?"

They stepped onto the half-empty dance-floor, turning slowly to the music. It was an old George Harrison song about God and Love. The musicians were pheezers who cared about the music. They did it justice.

"Do you love me, Cobb?"

The question caught him off guard. He hadn't loved anyone for years. He'd been too busy waiting to die. Love? He'd given it up when he left Verena alone in their apartment on Oglethorpe Street up in Savannah. But now . . .

"Why do you ask, Annie?"

"I've been living with you for a week." Her arms around his waist drew him closer. Her thighs. "And we still haven't made love. Is it that you're . . ."

"I'm not sure I remember how," Cobb said, not wanting to go into details. He wondered if there was an ERECTION subprogram in his library. Have to check on that later, have to find out what else was in there, too. He kissed Annie's cheek. "I'll do some research."

When the dance ended they sat down with Farker and his wife. The two were having a spat, you could tell from the claw-like way Cynthia was holding her fingers.

and from the confusion in Farker's eyes. They were glad to have Cobb and Annie interrupt them.

"What do you think of all this?" Cobb asked, using the hearty cheer-up-you-idiot tone he always used with Farker.

"Very nice," Cynthia Farker answered. "But there's no *streamers.*"

Emboldened by Cobb's presence, Farker waved over a waiter and ordered a pitcher of beer. Normally Cynthia wouldn't let him drink, not that he wanted to, normally, but this was, after all, the . . .

"Golden Prom," Annie said. "That's what we called it, since it's been about fifty years since a lot of us had our high-school Senior Prom. Do you remember yours, Cynthia?"

Cynthia lit a mentholated and lightly THC-ed cigarette. "Do I *remember?* Our class didn't *have* a prom. Instead some of the *hot*-heads on the student council voted to use the funds for a fall *bus*-trip."

"Where did you go?" Cobb asked.

Cynthia cackled shrilly. "To *Wash*ington! To march on the *Pent*agon! But it was worth it. That's where Farker and I met, isn't it dear."

Farker bobbed his light-bulb head in thought for a moment. "That's right. I was watching the Fugs chanting *Out Demon Out* on a flat-bed truck in the parking lot, and you stepped . . ."

"I didn't *step* on your foot, Farker. I *footsied* you. You looked like such an im*port*ant person with your *tape* recorder, and I was just *dying* to talk to you."

"You sure did," Farker said, grinning and shaking his head. "And you haven't stopped since."

The beer arrived then and they clinked glasses. Holding his glass up, Cobb closed his right nostril and took a snort. Sitting down, the dizziness was bearable. But, listening to his friends talk, he had a feeling of shame at no longer being human.

"How's your son?" he asked Cynthia, just to be saying something. Chuck, the Farkers' only child, was a United Cults minister up in Philadelphia. Cynthia loved to talk about him.

"He's getting more *nooky* than you ever saw!" Cynthia gave a thin cackle. "And the girls give him *money,* too. He teaches them astral pro*ject*ion."

"Some racket, huh?" Farker said, shaking his head. "If I were still young . . ."

"Not you," Annie said. "You're not psychic enough. But Cobb," she paused to smile at her escort, "Cobb could lead a cult any day."

"Well," Cobb said thoughtfully, "I have been feeling sort of psychic ever since . . ." He caught himself and skipped forward. "That is, I've been getting this feeling that the mind really *is* independent of your body. Even without your body, your mind could still exist as a sort of mathematical possibility. And telepathy is only . . ."

"That's just what *Chuck* says," Cynthia interrupted. "You must be getting *senile,* Cobb!"

They all laughed then, and started talking about other things: food and health and gossip. But, in the back of his mind, Cobb began thinking seriously about cults and religion.

The whole experience of changing bodies felt miraculous. Had he proved that the soul is real . . . or that it isn't? And there were his strange new flashes of empathy to explain. Was it that, having switched bodies once, he was no longer so matter-bound as before . . . or was it just the result of having mechanically sharp senses? What was he . . . guru or golem?

"You're cute," Annie said, and pulled him back onto the dance-floor.

Chapter Twenty-two

The Little Kidders put the robot that had looked like Sta-Hi in the back of the truck. Berdoo squeezed into the cab between Rainbow and Haf-N-Haf. No point taking a chance of her getting felt up.

"Thometimeth I wonder what Mr. Fwostee ith up to," Haf-N-Haf slobbered, pulling out onto the asphalt.

"That makes two of us, boah. But he pays cash."

"How much you got naow?" Rainbow asked, laying her hand on Berdoo's thigh. "Yew got enough to take me for a week at Disney World? And first Ah wanna baah me some new clothes and maybe change mah hayur."

"It looks real purty just lahk tis, Rainbow. Ah allus wanted me a cheap skank with green hair."

Berdoo and Haf-N-Haf began snickering, and Rainbow fell into a sulk. The truck ground over the Merrit Island Bridge, and then Haf-N-Haf turned right onto Route One. Night-bugs spattered against their windshield, and the hydrogen-fueled engine pocked away.

"Is Kristleen gonna git us a new monkey-man?" Berdoo asked after awhile.

"She'd bettew!" Haf-N-Haf answered, staring out past the headlights. "Filthy Phil ith on herw ath about it nonthop."

Berdoo shook his head. "Ah surely don't know whaah old Phil is so *waald* to be eatin brains all the time. It gets a little old, ya know?"

"Did he get Kristleen a new place to liyuv?" Rainbow wanted to know.

"Whah yew know he diyud, hunneh. Ain't nobody can bring in the troops lahk that Kristleen can."

"Well, Ah suhtainly hope that is a fact," Rainbow said primly. "Yew been promisin and promisin me a brain-feast and all Ah've done so far was almost git arreyusted."

"Ath wong ath Phil's wunnin the thow we'll be eating bwains," Haf-N-Haf assured her.

"Something right funny about ole Phil," Berdoo observed a bit later. "I ain't never seen him smoke nor take a drink nor eat any reglar food. And when he ain't givin orders he jest sits and stares."

They were in Daytona now, concrete and neon flickering past. Haf-N-Haf checked the mirror for cops, and then turned hard right into the Lido Hotel's underground garage. He parked the truck way in back, and plugged a wire into the wall-socket to keep the refrigeration unit running. A little camera eye poked out of a hole on the top of the truck. Anybody who came near the truck now would be hurting for sure. Mr. Frostee knew how to take care of himself, especially with his extra remote in back.

They took the elevator up to their suite. Filthy Phil was sitting there, shirt off, staring out the window at the moonlit sea. His fat back with its sagging tattoo was facing them. He didn't bother to turn around.

"*Notice to Satan:*" Rainbow said, shrilly reading Phil's back aloud. "*Send this Man to Heaven, Cause He's Done His Time in Hell.*" She read it in her dumbest schoolgirl tone. She didn't like Phil.

Phil still didn't turn around. Once there had been a human Filthy Phil, a welder who worked too late on BEX up at Ledge one nightshift. BEX had put the brain-tape in charge of his humanoid repair robot . . . but it hadn't worked out. The personality had flattened out to that of an affectless killer. But he was still a good mechanic.

When they'd decided to send Mr. Frostee down to start collecting souls, Phil had come with him. Mr. Frostee still used Phil's brain-tape when he needed repairs. But he didn't like to put the personality in charge of the robot unless he had to. So, as a rule, the robot-remote

called Filthy Phil had all the warmth and human respon-
siveness of a pair of vice-grip pliers.

"Y'all leave Phil alone," Berdoo warned Rainbow.
"He's waitin for the phone to ring, ain't that right,
Phil?"

Phil nodded curtly. The shuttle to BEX was taking off
tomorrow, and Phil Frostee had promised to send up a
new set of organs. A tape could go up anytime, by radio
. . . but he'd promised a whole person, body and soul,
hardware and software. If Kristleen didn't find someone
. . . He stared out the window, listening to the three human voices behind him, and making his plans.

The phone rang then. Phil sprang across the room and
snatched it up.

"Filthy Phil."

The voice on the other end was high-pitched, tearful.
Berdoo looked at Haf-N-Haf nervously. Even through the
mirror-shades you could see that Phil was mad. But his
voice came out smooth.

"I understand, Kristleen. Yes I understand. O.K.
Fine."

More talking from the other end. Slowly a smile spread
on Phil's muscular face. He looked over at Berdoo and
winked.

"O.K. Kristleen. If he's asleep why don't you just
come over now and we can pay you off. You got five
grand coming. You better come get it now, because
we're going to shift bases tomorrow. Right. That's right.
O.K., baby. And don't worry, I do understand."

Phil set the phone down gently, almost tenderly.
"Kristleen's in love. She just blew a college boy and
now she's sitting there watching him sleep. He sleeps
like a baby, she says, like an innocent child." Phil began walking around the room, moving pieces of furniture
this way and that.

"Kwithtween'th not going to dewiver and you're going
to pay herw off anyway?" Haf-N-Haf asked incredu-
lously.

"That's what I told her," Phil said evenly, "but I'm
in a tight spot. I've got to have a body by tomorrow
morning. The tape could go any time, but I've got a

cargo-slot all signed up and paid for.'' He took a small sleep-dart pistol out of a drawer and examined it carefully.

"You ain't gonna kill Kristleen?'' Rainbow cried.

"It's not really killing,'' Phil said, holding the pistol half-raised. "Haven't you figured that out yet? Berdoo?''

Berdoo felt like he was back in eighth grade, being asked questions he couldn't begin to understand. "Ah donno, Phil. It's yore gang. Yew got the truck and the apartment and all. Ah'll help you snuff Kristleen.'' If he weren't a Little Kidder he'd be nothing again.

"We'll eat her brain,'' Phil said, spinning the pistol and watching them closely. "But her thoughts will live on.'' With his left hand he poked abruptly at his chest. "Look!''

A little door swung open, showing the inside of a metal compartment in his chest. There were knives in there, and little machines. It looked like a tiny laboratory.

Rainbow screamed and Berdoo stepped over to cover her mouth. Haf-N-Haf made a noise that might have been a laugh.

"I'm part of Mr. Frostee,'' Phil explained, snapping the door back shut. "I'm like his hand, you wave? Or his mouth.'' Phil smiled broadly then, revealing his strong, sharp teeth. "We boppers use human organs to seed our tissue farms. We use brain-tapes for simulators in some of our robot-remotes. Like me. And we just like brains anyhow, even the ones we don't actually use. A human mind is a beautiful thing.''

"Well you kin leave us out!'' Rainbow cried. "Ah'll be buggered befo ah help yew!''

"Shut up, fool,'' Berdoo snarled at her. "Ah buggered yew yestidday, yew should recall.''

"Ah am *not* gonna stand baah and let . . .'' Rainbow began.

The doorbell cut her off in mid cry. Phil aimed the sleep-dart gun at Rainbow.

"Are you going to let Kristleen in, Rainbow? Or should I use you instead?''

Rainbow went to the door and opened it for Kristleen. Standing across the room, Phil was able to nail the two women with two quick shots. The sleep-drug took effect and they collapsed. Haf-N-Haf dragged them in and closed the door.

Berdoo stood watching, miserable and confused. Rainbow was the only girl-friend he'd ever had. But Phil had always been right before. Phil was Mr. Frostee, really. And Mr. Frostee was smarter than anyone in the world.

"She's going to make trouble if we let her go, Berdoo." Phil was looking at him across the room, his gun still levelled. There was a silence.

"But ah *cayun't!*" Berdoo cried finally. "Not that sweet girl. Ah *cain't* let you cut her all . . ."

Suddenly there was a pistol in Berdoo's hand, a .38 special. Faster than thought, his street-fighter's reflexes had carried him over to the window and fanned the drape out in front of him. Phil's sleep-dart bounced off the drape and dropped to the floor.

"Be reasonable, Berdoo." Phil lowered his dart pistol. "We'll take Kristleen apart, but we'll send Rainbow up whole. She can work for BEX as a stewardess, to re-place that girl Misty from last year. Now you just let me get Rainbow stoned up good, and I'll talk to her, and then she flies up to Disky and gets herself an ever-lasting body. I promise they'll leave her personality in. You'll be able to see her once in a . . ."

Berdoo stepped out from behind the curtain, his small face set in a snarl. He shot Phil through the head, just like that.

"Oh, Bewdoo," Haf-N-Haf moaned as the ringing of the pistol-shot died down. "We're going to have to wun wike hell. Mr. Fwostee's got that other wemote in the twuck!"

"We'll go out front and steal us a car," Berdoo said tersely. "Ah'll drag Rainbow, an you handle Kristleen."

Just as they left the room, something in there exploded. Phil's body? They didn't stop to find out. Staggering under the women's dead weight, they bumped down the fire-stairs and out through the lobby.

An athletic young man was just parking a red convertible in front. Berdoo still had his pistol out. Haf-N-Haf tapped the man's shoulder and said something. He looked them over, handed over the keys, and backed off without saying a thing. Haf-N-Haf and Berdoo often affected people that way.

They put the girls in back and took off for the thruway to Orlando.

Chapter Twenty-three

The Golden Prom was a lot of fun. Cobb hadn't en-joyed himself so much in years. The beauty of the DRUNKENNESS subprogram was that you could move your intoxication level up and down at will, instead of being caught on a relentless down escalator to bargain basement philosophy and the parking garage. He found that if he tried to go further than ten drinks, to the black-out point, then an automatic over-ride would cut in and he'd loop back to where he started.

Leaving the dance with Annie, he took a few sobering right-nostril breaths and wrapped his arm around her waist. She was acting girlish and giggly.

"Have you finished your research, Cobb?"

"What." The moon was hanging over the sea now. Its light made a long lapped lane of gold, leading out to the edge of the world. "What research?"

She slipped her hand into his pants in back and smoothed his buttock. "*You* know."

"That's right," Cobb said. "Be-boppa-lu-la."

"Library accessed," a voice in his head said.

"I want to have sex."

"I'm glad," Annie said. "So do I."

"SEX subroutine now activated," the voice said.

"OUT," Cobb said.

"It's out?" Annie asked. "I thought you wanted to."

Cobb felt his pants tightening in front. "I do, I do."

They stopped once or twice to kiss and rub against each other. Every square centimeter of Cobb's body tin-gled with anticipation. For the first time in years his whole consciousness was out on his skin. Out on both their skins, really, for when they kissed he felt himself merging into Annie's personality. One flesh.

For some reason the lights in his cottage were on. At first he thought it had just been an oversight . . . but walking up to the door he heard Sta-Hi's voice.

"Oh," Annie cried happily. "How wonderful! Your friend is better again!"

Cobb followed her into his cottage. Sta-Hi and Mooney were sitting there arguing. They fell silent when they saw Cobb and Annie.

Annie was angry to see Mooney there again. "What do you want, pig?"

Mooney didn't say anything, but just leaned back in Cobb's easy chair, his alert eyes looking the old man up and down.

"It is really you, Sta-Hi?" Cobb asked. "Did they beam you down or . . ."

"It's the real me," Sta-Hi said. "All-meat. I came back on the shuttle today. How was *your* trip?"

"You would have loved it. I couldn't tell yes from no." Cobb started to say more, then stopped himself. It wasn't clear how much it would be safe to let Mooney know. Had they found the switched-off robot in the bedroom? Then he noticed the pistol in Mooney's lap.

"Maybe you should send the lady home," Mooney suggested easily. "I think we have some things to talk over."

"SEX OUT," Cobb muttered bitterly, "DRUNKENNESS OUT. You better go, Annie. Mr. Mooney's right."

"But why should I? I live here now, too. Who does this crummy Gimmie loach think he is, making me leave?" She was close to tears. "And after such a wonderful evening, just when . . ."

Cobb put his arm around her and walked her out the door. Patches of light from his cottage windows lay on the crushed-shell driveway. He could see Mooney's alert shadow in one of the windows.

"Don't worry, Annie. I'll make it up to you tomorrow. Suddenly it's like . . . like life is starting all over again."

"But what do they want? Have you done something wrong? Do they have a right to arrest you?"

Cobb thought a minute. Conceivably they could have him dismantled as a bopper spy. As a machine, he probably wouldn't even be entitled to a trial. But there was no reason it had to come to that. He put his arms around Annie and gave her a last kiss.

"I'll talk to them. I'll talk my way out. Save a place for me in your bed. I might be over in a half-hour."

"All right," Annie breathed in his ear. "And I've got a gun too, you know. I'll watch out the window in case . . ."

Cobb hugged her tighter, whispering back, "Don't do that, honey. I can handle them. If worst comes to worst I'll . . . skip out. But . . ."

"Come on, Anderson," Mooney called from Cobb's window. "We're waiting to talk to you."

Cobb and Annie exchanged a last hand-squeeze, and Cobb went back in his house. He sat down in the easy chair that Mooney had been using, leaving Mooney to lean against the wall and glower at him, pistol in hand. Sta-Hi was lounging in a deck-chair he'd dragged in, a lit reefer in his mouth.

"Start talking, Anderson," Mooney said. He was keeping the pistol aimed at Cobb's head. A body shot probably wouldn't stop a robot, but . . .

"Take it easy, Dad," Sta-Hi put in. "Cobb's not going to hurt anyone."

"You let me be a judge of that, Stanny. For all we know, that other robot is hiding right outside to help him."

"What robot?" Cobb said. How much did they really know, anyway? He and Sta-Hi had split up before the operation, and . . .

"Look," Sta-Hi said, a little wearily. "Let's cut the noise-level. I *know* that you're a machine now, Cobb. The boppers put you in your robot-double. Stuzzy! I can wave with it. The only problem is that my father here . . .''

The old hard-cop/soft-cop routine. Cobb abandoned his first line of defense and asked for information.

''Where's the Sta-Hi$_2$ robot?''

''The Little Kidders were here,'' Sta-Hi said. ''They carried the robot out of your bedroom and left. It looked like they were driving an ice-cream truck.''

''Mr. Frostee,'' Cobb said absently. He was thinking hard. What the boppers had done to him was, on the whole, a good thing. A whole nother ball-game. If only he could make Sta-Hi and Mooney see . . .

''Where's your base of operations?'' Mooney demanded. ''How many others like you are there?'' He gestured menacingly with his pistol.

Cobb shrugged. ''Don't ask me. The boppers never tell me anything. I'm just a poor old man with an artificial body.'' He looked over at Sta-Hi for sympathy. As with Annie before, he was getting a telepathic feeling, a feeling that he could see through the two other men's eyes. Sta-Hi was stoned, receptive and open to change. But Mooney was tense and frightened.

''As far as I know,'' Cobb said, ''I'm completely in control of myself. I don't think the boppers plan to use me as a remote-control robot or anything like that.''

''What's in it for them?'' Mooney asked.

''They said they wanted to do me a favor,'' Cobb said. He considered opening his food-unit door to show Mooney the letter, but then thought better of it. But thinking of the door suggested a possibility.

''Be-boppa-lu-la,'' Cobb said out loud.

''Library accessed.''

''Was there a subroutine called MR. FROSTEE?''

''Now activated,'' the voice murmured.

Something opened up in Cobb's mind, and a whole different set of visual stimuli overlaid the yellowed walls of his living-room.

He was still in his cottage, yet he was also in a concrete parking garage. Something very bad had just happened. Berdoo had shot Phil, his best remote. It was like losing an eye. And now there was no way to see what

Berdoo and Haf-N-Haf were doing. Should he send the extra remote after them?

"Hello," Cobb thought, stopping himself from saying the word aloud.

"Cobb?" Mr. Frostee's response was quick and unsurprised. "I was hoping to talk to you. But I wanted to let you make the first move. We don't want you to feel . . ."

"Like a remote?"

"Right. You're designed for full autonomy, Cobb. If you can help us, so much the better. But there's no way we would have edited out your freewill . . . even if we knew how. You're still entirely your own man."

"What do you want from me?" Silently asking this, Cobb leaned back in his chair, stretching out his legs. Mooney looked impatient. Sta-Hi was staring at the bugs on the ceiling.

"Convince the others," came Mr. Frostee's reply. In the background, Cobb could make out the interior of a truck-cab. Hands on the steering wheel. The concrete walls of a parking garage, then the garish lights of Daytona Beach streaming past.

"Convince them all to get robot bodies like you. Then we can merge, we can *all* merge to become a new and greater being. We'll set up a number of reprocessing centers . . ."

Mooney was standing over Cobb, shaking him. It was hard to see, with the glare of headlights coming at him. Slowly, Cobb brought his attention back to the cottage.

"What's the matter, Mooney?"

"You're signalling for help, aren't you?"

"How would you like a nice ever-lasting body like mine?" Cobb countered. "I could arrange it."

"So that's it," Sta-Hi said dreamily. "The big boppers want to bring us *all* into the fold."

"It's not so unreasonable," Cobb protested. "It's a natural next evolutionary step. Imagine people that carry mega-byte computing systems in their head, people that communicate directly brain-to-brain, people who live for centuries and change bodies like suits of clothes!"

"Imagine people that aren't people," Sta-Hi replied. "Cobb, the big boppers like TEX and MEX have been trying to run the same con on the Moon. And most of the little boppers up there aren't buying it . . . most would rather fight then let themselves be patched into the big systems. Now why do you think that is?"

"Obviously some people . . . or boppers . . . are going to be paranoid about losing their precious individuality," Cobb answered. "But that's just a matter of cultural conditioning! Look, Sta-Hi, I've been all the way in . . . *all* the way. After I got taped on the Moon I was just a pattern in a memory-bank somewhere for a few days. And you know, it wasn't even that . . ."

"Let's go," Mooney ordered, roughly pulling Cobb to his feet. "You're going to be deprogrammed and dismantled, Anderson. We can't let this kind of . . ."

Mr. Frostee was still there in Cobb's head. "I've taken the liberty of activating your SELF-DESTRUCT subroutine," the voice said quietly. "Just say the word 'DESTROY' out loud and you'll explode. Your body will explode. *You're* really in me. I'll give you a new body, the one here in the truck . . ."

"MR. FROSTEE OUT," Cobb said. If he did it, he wanted it to be his own decision.

Mooney had his pistol at the base of Cobb's skull. He was getting panicky.

Any second, Mooney, Cobb thought to himself. But still he hesitated. He told himself it was just because he didn't want to hurt Sta-Hi . . . but he was also scared, scared to die again. Could he really cross the noisy void between bodies again? But he'd already done it once, hadn't he?

"Go outside, Sta-Hi," Mooney said then, and sealed his fate. "Go check if that old bitch is waiting out there to ambush us. Or the other robot."

Sta-Hi eased out the back door and melted into the night.

"I've finally got you," Mooney said, with a nudge of his pistol. "I'm going to find out what makes you tick."

"DESTROY," Cobb said, and lost his second body.

Chapter Twenty-four

"I want to talk to you about diarrhea," a voice said earnestly. "Gastric distress can *ruin* that long-hoped-for vacation. So be sure . . ."

Cobb's first conscious act was to turn the radio off. He had just pulled out of a fuel-station on the gritty outskirts of Daytona Beach. But, on the other hand, he had just died in the explosion of his cottage in Cocoa Beach.

"Hello, Cobb. You see? You can count on me." Mr. Frostee's voice filled his head again. Cobb looked down at his sinewy forearms, handling the ice-cream truck's big steering-wheel with an experienced touch.

"Sta-Hi$_2$?" Cobb asked. "You put me in Sta-Hi$_2$?"

"It *was* Sta-Hi$_2$ But I just gave the body a new look. I copied the fellow who was running the pumps back there."

Cobb thought back to the explosion. DESTROY, disorientation, and now this. His fingers were blackened with years of grease. He leaned out the window to take a peek at himself in the rearview mirror.

He had a skinny head and large, liquid eyes. Thinning black hair, greasy and combed straight back. His nose was much more prominent than his chin. Ratface. Approaching headlights pulled his attention back to the road.

"What about disguising the truck?" Cobb asked. "I killed Mooney, but he must have left records. And Sta-Hi got away. The heat's gonna be looking for a Mr. Frostee truck."

"There'll be time for that later. Right now I've got a score to settle. Those hoodlums . . . those Little Kidders

. . . one of them wrecked my best remote. He's called Berdoo.''

Without consciously thinking about it, Cobb had driven the truck onto the thruway west, towards Orlando. Was he still in control of his actions?

"Where are we going?"

"Disney World. Berdoo doesn't remember it, but he once told me . . . told Phil . . . that he has a friend who runs a motel there. I think that's where he'll go to hide out. I want you to shoot him, Cobb, and then take out his brain for me. We'll leave the organs . . . that's all over for now . . . but I've got to get that brain on tape. You should have seen how easily he killed my Phil.''

It was hard to read the emotion in Mr. Frostee's even voice. Was revenge the motive? Or was it just a collector's lust for ownership?

In any case, trying to ambush the Little Kidders in their own hideout sounded like a terrible idea. And going brain-collecting was something Cobb hoped to put off as long as possible. He wondered if he should just turn around. Or pull off the highway and leave the truck. Glancing in his rear-view mirror he could see dawn pinkening the horizon. The road was empty.

"You've still got your free will," Mr. Frostee said. "But don't forget that we're in this together. If I die then so do you. You're really just a pattern in my circuits.''

"But you can't override me?" Testing, Cobb took his foot off the accelerator. No one pushed his foot back.

"I can't control your mind," Mr. Frostee said, not quite answering the question. "But don't stop the truck. What if a cop comes by?''

Cobb speeded back up. "Why would you give one of your subsystems free will?''

"The human mind is all of a piece, Cobb. If we try to start picking and choosing, all that's left is a boring bundle of reflexes. When a big bopper builds in some human's personality, he's got to learn to live with the subsystem's free will. I *could* cut you off entirely, in an emergency, but short of . . .''

"Why bother taping humans at all?''

"No program we can write and control acts like human software. Humans can't write bopper programs . . . they had to let them evolve. And a bopper can't write a human program. It works both ways. We need you guys. What we're working towards is a human-bopper fusion, a single great mind stretching from person to person all over the world. It's right, Cobb, and it's inevitable. Simpler beings merge to produce higher beings, and they must merge and merge again. In this way we draw ever closer to the One."

"*The One?*" Cobb said, laughing. "You don't mean the One on the Moon, do you? Don't you know that's just a random noise source? Haven't you figured that out?"

"*Randomness* is an elusive concept, Cobb."

"Look," Cobb said, "In order to make the boppers evolve fast enough I had to speed up the rate of mutation. So in the substrate program I included a command that they plug into the One, once a month, as you know.

"But the One is just a simple cosmic ray counter. It goes through your programs changing yesses and noes, here and there, just on the basis of the geigercounter click-pattern of cosmic-ray bursts for the last day or so. The One is just a glorified circuit-scrambler."

Still Mr. Frostee was silent. Finally the answer came. "You choose to make light of the One, Cobb. But the pulse of the One is the pulse of the Cosmos. You yourself call its noisy input the *cosmic rays*. What is more natural than that the Cosmos should lovingly direct the growth of the boppers with its bursts of radiation? There is no *noise* in the All . . . there is only *information*. Nothing is truly random. It is sad that you choose not to understand what you yourself have created."

A ditch full of brackish water and marsh-grass lay to the right of the thruway. Cobb saw an alligator, lying half out of the water and watching the early morning traffic. It was quarter to seven. In a sort of phantom-stomach reflex, Cobb had a brief longing for breakfast. But the hunger faded, and Cobb let the empty miles roll by, lost in thought.

What was he now? In one sense he was what he had always been. A certain pattern, a type of software. The *fiveness* of a right hand is the same as the *fiveness* of a left. The *Cobbness* that had been a man was the same as the *Cobbness* now coded upon Mr. Frostee's cold chips.

Cobb Anderson's brain had been dissected, but the software that made up his mind had been preserved. The idea of "self" is, after all, just another idea, a symbol in the software. Cobb felt like him *self* as much as ever. And, as much as ever, Cobb wanted his self to continue to exist on hardware.

Perhaps the boppers had stored a tape of him on the Moon, and perhaps up there his software had also been given hardware. But, here and now, Cobb's continued existence depended on keeping Mr. Frostee cold and energized. They were in this together. Him and a machine who wanted to know God.

"I'll tell you," Cobb said, breaking the silence. "I think it would be really stupid to go charging after the Little Kidders before getting the truck repainted. Even if the cops aren't after us yet, there's no point having Berdoo be able to see you coming from a block away. Let's get off the thruway and fix up the truck. There's a giant plastic ice-cream cone on the cab's roof, for God's sake."

"You're driving," Mr. Frostee said mildly. "I will defer to your superior knowledge of human criminality."

Cobb got out at the next exit and took a small road north. This was rolling countryside, with plenty of streams. Palms and magnolias gave way to blackjack pines and scrubby live oak. Brambles and honeysuckle filled in the spaces between the struggling little trees. And in some places the uncontrollable kudzu vine had taken root and choked out all other vegetation.

It was only eight-thirty, but already the asphalt road was shimmering in the heat. The frequent dips were filled with reflecting water-mirages. Cobb rolled down the window and let the air beat against his face. The truck's big hydrogen-fueled engine roared smoothly and the sticky road sang beneath the tires.

The wild scrub gave way to farmland, big cleared pastures with cattle in them. The cows waded about knee-deep in weeds, munching the flowers. White cattle egrets stalked and flapped along next to them, spearing the insects that the cows stirred up. The egrets looked like little old men with no arms.

A few miles of pastures and barns brought them to a bend in the road called Purcell. There were some big houses and some cracker-boxes, a tiny Winn-Dixie, and a couple of fuel-stations. Cobb pulled into a tree-shaded Hy-Gas that had a handpainted sign saying *Body Work*.

There was a three-legged dog lying on the asphalt by the pumps. When Cobb pulled up, the animal rose and limped off, barking. The fourth leg ended half-way down, in a badly bandaged stub.

Cobb hopped out of the truck cab. A young sandy-haired man in stained white coveralls came ambling out of the garage. He had prominent ears and thick lips.

"Mr. Frostee taahm!" the attendant observed. He screwed the hydrogen nozzle into the truck's hydride tanks. There was a sort of foliated metal in the tanks which could absorb several hundred liters of the gas. "Gimme one?"

"It's empty," Cobb said. "This isn't really a Mr. Frostee truck anymore. It's mine."

The attendant absorbed this fact in silence, looking Cobb's skinny ratfaced body up and down. "You baah it?"

"I sure did," Cobb said. "Over in Cocoa. Fella closed his franchise down. I aim to fix this truck up and use it for my meat business."

The attendant topped up the tank. He was tanned, with white squint-wrinkles around his eyes. He shot Cobb a sharp glance.

"You don't look lahk no butcher to me. You look lahk a grease-monkey in a stolen truck." He punctuated this with a sudden, toothy smile. "But ah could be wrong. You need anything besides the hydrogen?"

The guy was suspicious, but seemed willing to be bought off. Cobb decided to stay. "Actually . . . I'd like to get this truck painted. It's a burden having to explain to everyone that it's really mine."

"Ah reckon *so,*" the sandy-haired man said, smiling broadly. "If you pull her round back, Ah maaht could he'p you solve your problems. Ah'll paint it and forget it. Cost you a thousand dollahs."

That was much too high for two hours' work. The guy obviously thought the truck was stolen.

"O.K.," Cobb said, meeting the other man's prying eyes. "But don't try to double-cross me."

The attendant displayed his many crooked teeth in another smile. "What color y'all want?"

"Paint it black," Cobb said, relishing the old phrase. "But first let's get that goddamn cone off the top."

He got back in the truck, pulled off the asphalt, and drove through rutted weeds to the junky lot behind the Hy-Gas station. The attendant, on foot, led the way.

"Perhaps he is not honest," Mr. Frostee said inside Cobb's head, sounding a bit worried.

"Of course he isn't," Cobb answered. "What we have to look out for is him calling the cops anyway, or trying to blackmail us for more money."

"I think you should kill him and eat his brain," Mr. Frostee said quickly.

"That's not the answer to *every* problem in interpersonal relations," Cobb said, hopping out. He was learning to talk to Mr. Frostee subvocally, without actually opening his mouth.

The attendant had brought a screwdriver and a couple of Lock-Tite wrenches. He and Cobb got the cone off, after ten or fifteen minutes' work. The emptily smiling swirl-topped face landed in the weeds next to half of a rusted-out motorcycle. The two men's bodies worked well together, and a certain sympathy developed between them.

The attendant introduced himself as Jody Doakes. Cobb, hoping to confuse his trail, said his name was Berdoo. They went around front to get the paint and the spray-gun compressor. Cobb solved the problem of when to pay, by tearing a thousand-dollar-bill in half and giving Jody one piece.

"You'll get the other half when I pull out of here," Cobb said. "And no earlier."

"Ah see yore point," Jody said, with a knowing chuckle.

First they had to wash the truck off. Then they taped newspaper over the tires, lights and windows. They sprayed everything else black. The paint dried fast in the hot air. They were able to start the second coat as soon as they finished the first.

The job took all morning. Now and then that three-legged dog would start barking, and Jody would go out to serve a customer. Mr. Frostee's refrigeration unit kept running, drawing its energy from the hydride tank. Jody asked once why the refrigerator had to be on if there wasn't any more ice-cream. Cobb told him that if he wanted the other half of the thousand-dollar-bill he could keep his questions to himself.

They finished the second coat a few minutes after the noon siren blew on the Purcell fire-house.

"Y'all want a baaht to eat?" Jody asked. "Ah got the makins for sandwiches insahd." He hooked his thumb at the garage.

"Sure," Cobb said, ignoring the fact that he'd just have to clean the chewed-up bread and lunchmeat out of his food unit later on. Eating was fun. "I could use a couple of beers, too."

"Come shot!" Jody said, meaning something like *you bet*. "Come shot on the beer, Berdoo."

They had a friendly lunch. More strongly than ever, Cobb felt able to enter into other people's thoughts. Again the thought of starting a cult crossed his mind.

The food and beer felt good in his mouth. Over Mr. Frostee's protests, Cobb cut in the DRUNKENNESS subroutine and gave himself a hit for each beer. They split a six-pack. Jody allowed as how, for an extra two hundred bucks, he'd be willing to let Cobb have some fresh license plates and registration papers he happened to have.

Cobb enjoyed their dealings very much. In his old body he had never been able to talk comfortably to garage mechanics. But now, with a random grease-monkey's face on a Sta-Hi-shaped body, Cobb fit in at a filling station as easily as he used to fit in at research labs. Idly he wondered if Mr. Frostee could change the flicker-cladding enough to turn him into a woman. That would be interesting. There was so much to look forward to!

After lunch they changed the license plates. Cobb handed over the missing half of the thousand-dollar-bill, and the extra two hundred dollars. Hoping to keep Jody bought, he suggested that he might be back with more of the same kind of business next month, if things worked out.

"Come shot!" Jody said. "And good luck."

Cobb drove out of Purcell, heading east, past cows and egrets.

"I wish you'd taped his brain," Mr. Frostee nagged. "We can always use a good mechanic."

Cobb had been expecting a remark like this. And the next remark, too.

"How come you're driving East? That's not the right way to Disney World. We've still got to get Berdoo!"

"Mr. Frostee," Cobb said, "I love my new body. And I support your basic plan. It's the logical next step for human evolution. But mass-murder is not the way. There's a better way, a way to get people to *volunteer* for brain-taping. We'll start a new religious cult!"

There was a pained silence. Finally Mister Frostee spoke. "I feel I should warn you, Cobb. You have free will in the sense that I can't control your thoughts. But the body belongs to *both* of us. In certain special circumstances I may take . . ."

"Please," Cobb said, "hear me out. Am I right in believing that you're the only big bopper now on Earth?"

"That's right."

"And I'm using the only robot-remote you have left?"

"Yes. Hopefully, with Mooney out of the way, security at the spaceport will be relaxed again. We had planned a shipment of some thousand new remotes during the next two years, as well as several more big bopper units. These plans are unfortunately . . . in flux. There are some . . . difficulties on the Moon. But until the situation restabilizes, I intend to continue gathering tapes and . . ."

"You're trying to tell me there's an all-out civil war starting on the Moon, aren't you?" Cobb exclaimed. "We're on our own, M.F.! If we go back to the spaceport and try . . ."

"There is no need to go to spaceport for tape transmission. I can radio-beam the tapes directly up to BEX at Ledge."

"A soul transmitter," Cobb said thoughtfully. "That's a good angle. *Personetics: The Science of Immortality.*"

"What do you mean?"

"The religion! We'll get the down-and-out, the runaways, the culties . . . we'll get them to believe that you're a machine for sending their souls to heaven. It's not really so . . ."

"But why bother? Why not just proceed as Phil always did. To *seize*, and cut, and . . ."

"Look, M.F., we're in this together. It works both ways. If something happens to this truck I'm dead. I don't think you realize just how strongly humans react to murder and cannibalism. This is no bopper *anarchy* here, it's more like a *police*-state. If you and I are going to last out until BEX gets the troops here, we're going to need to lay low and play it careful."

Just thinking about it gave Cobb the creeps. If he couldn't get fuel for the truck, if the cops stopped them, if the refrigeration unit broke . . . It was like being a snail with a ten-ton shell! A snowball in hell!

"We need security," Cobb said urgently. "We need a lot of people to take care of us, and we need money to keep the hydride tanks full. If we get enough money I think we should build a scion, too. A copy of your processor. We could get our followers to buy the components in computer shops. You've got to understand the realities of life on Earth!"

"All right," Mr. Frostee said finally. "I agree. But where are you driving to?"

"Back to the coast," Cobb said. "I know a place north of Daytona Beach where we can hole up. And, say . . . give me a new face. Something fatherly."

Chapter Twenty-five

After his father's funeral, Sta-Hi went back to driving a cab in Daytona Beach. Bea, his mother, wanted to put the house up for sale and move north, away from the pheezers. She hated them since Mooney's death . . . and who could blame her! Her husband had gone to old Cobb Anderson's house on a routine check, and had been blown to smithereens! Just for doing his job! And so on.

There was an investigation into Mooney's death, but the blast hadn't left a hell of a lot to investigate. There was not a scrap of the suspected robot double to be found. And Sta-Hi didn't tell the authorities any more than he had to. He still couldn't decide whose side he was on.

He took a couple of his father's space-ship paintings and rented a room in Daytona. He went back to Yellow Cab and they gave him a job driving the night-shift. Mostly it was a matter of bringing drunks and whores to motels. Seamy. And duller'n shit.

His dope habit crept up on him again. Pretty soon he was smoking, snorting, dropping, spraying and shooting his money as fast as he made it. Late at night, driving up and down the one-dimensional city, Sta-Hi would dream and scheme, forming huge, interlocking plans for the future.

He would make a movie about cab-driving. He would write a book about the boppers. No, man, do it with music!

He would learn how to play the guitar and start a band. Fuck learning! He would get another Happy Cloak and let it play his fingers for him. He needed a Happy Cloak!

He'd threaten the boppers to tell about the Little Kidders and the nursies if they wouldn't come across. With Anderson and his father blown up, no one else knew!

He'd get rich and then go back to Disky and get in on the civil war and they'd make him king. Hadn't he already helped the diggers to off a big bopper? He'd lead them to victory! Moon King Sta-Hi!

But there was no way to reach the boppers. The cops had lost track of Mr. Frostee and those Little Kidders. BEX and Misty-girl never got any closer to Earth than space-station Ledge. And no private phone-calls to Disky were allowed. The thing to do was to make the boppers contact *him*. How? Get so famous they'd notice him!

Around and around, night after night, tripping and bouncing the length of dreary Daytona. One night a drunk left his wallet in the cab. Two thousand bucks in there. Sta-Hi took the money and quit work. He needed time to think!

He got a crate of Z-gas aerosols . . . he'd sunken that low . . . and started hanging around the strip. Eating burgers, selling hits, playing machines, hunting pussy. He tried to make himself conspicuous, hoping something would happen to him. The day his money ran out, it finally did.

He was hanging out at Hideo-Nuts' Boltsadrome, stoned, staring at the floor. His boots looked so perfect. Two dark parabolas in a field of yellow, slight 3-D interest provided by the scurf strewn about. His favorite song was playing. He felt like screaming, like crying out, "I'm here and I'm staying high! I'm Sta-Hi, the king of the brainsurfers!"

The metal speaker overhead was pumping out solid music. He could see the notes if he squinted. He started to giggle, thinking of the tiny note-shaped bumps travelling down the wires like white mice swallowed by a python. God, he had good ideas!

Keeping his smile, in case it came in handy, Sta-Hi looked around the arcade, swaying back and forth, fingering chords on an invisible electric guitar. He couldn't

actually play yet, but he had all the moves down . . .
say . . . look at little blondie over there. He stared at
her and slid a riff down the neck of his imaginary guitar.
Smiling harder, he beckoned with his head.

Liking his smile, the broad-hipped girl strolled towards him, swaying back and forth like a slowly swim-
ming fish. *Beat* that tail. She kept her head tilted back
to show off the tan-stars on her cheeks.

"Hi 'surfer. God, it's wiggly in here tonight." She
shook back her hair and laughed a slow, knowing laugh.
"I'm Wendy."

Sta-Hi sizzled off a few more hot chords and then
threw his hands in the air. "You're talking to Sta-Hi
Mooney, fluffy. I've got the weenie, you've got the bun,
put em together and have some gum." His rap had de-
teriorated badly during the last week of Z-gas.

"Are you in a club?" Wendy asked, still smiling. He
wasn't as stuzzy as she had thought from across the
room. And, worse, he looked broke.

"Sure . . . I mean practically." She wasn't really as
pretty as he had thought. A whore? "How about you?"

"Oh I've been hanging out . . . parties . . . burning
cars. . . ." Wendy wondered if it was worth wasting
time on him. She had to make five hundred dollars before going back to the temple.

Sta-Hi saw the doubt in Wendy's face. She was the
first girl he'd managed to talk to all day. He was going
to have to land this fish, and fast. "Have a whiff on
me," he said, fumbling out his aerosol.

"Wiggly," she said, tossing her hair again. He handed
her the little can and she inhaled a short burst of the
Z-gas. Sta-Hi took it back and blasted off a long, long
one. Gongs rang in his ears and he staggered a little,
laughing a hyuck-hyuck 'surfer laugh from the back of
his throat. Wendy took the can out of his hand and hit
up another. They looked pretty to each other again.

"What do you want to play?" Sta-Hi asked, gesturing
broadly.

"I'm good in that *Pleasure Garden*," Wendy answered.

"Wiggly." Sta-Hi dropped his last five-dollar coin into the slot. The big machine lit up and made a googly welcome-to-my-nightmare noise.

"I'll do the pushpads," Wendy said, taking her place in front of the machine.

That was fine with Sta-Hi. He'd never gotten too good at playing the hyperpins. He took the electron-gun in his hand and pushed the start button.

A little silver ball popped into play. A magnetic field buoyed it up. Sta-Hi aimed the gun at the ball and gave it a kick towards the first target.

He'd shot it the wrong way, though, and it disappeared into a trap . . . the mouth in a glowing little Shiva. Wendy gave a snort of annoyance. Wordlessly, Sta-Hi punched the start again.

This time he sent the ball right into the nearest pushpad. Let her handle it. She did . . . banking the chrome sphere off two more pads before sending it edgewise down a whole row of pop-ups.

"Stuzzy," Sta-Hi breathed. They were both leaning over the lit-up tank. First you had to take out fifteen targets and then the Specials would light up. Wendy had just gotten five targets at once. The ball was drifting towards a trap, but Sta-Hi managed to shoot it in time. Then Wendy was batting it around with the push-pads again.

She had a long, chiming run. All the specials were lit now. Asserting himself, Sta-Hi flicked the ball a few times with the electron-gun, trying to knock it down one of the money holes. But they had repellers, and he ended up by pushing the ball out.

"Have you ever played this before?" Wendy wanted to know before he launched their last ball.

"I'm sorry. I guess I'm a little phased."

"Don't apologize. We're doing good. But on this next ball could you sort of . . . just shoot when I say to?"

"I'll shoot when and where you like, baby." He pressed the start and slid his hand down to pat her ass, knowing she couldn't let go of the controls to slap him away. But she didn't even frown . . . just bumped her tummy against the machine and whispered, "Shoot."

Sta-Hi shot and they were off. She pushed the pads, murmuring instructions to him all the while. *Down, farther, watch the crocs, give it to me, hit the pad, way down* . . . They took out all the targets and all the level-one specials. Then they were working on the higher-level specials. The traps were moving around, snapping at the ball, and Wendy was making impossible saves. Sta-Hi's finger was clenched tight on the trigger.

The machine was letting out wild wheeps and rings, and a few people drifted over to watch Sta-Hi and Wendy work out. Faster, tighter angles, shooting constantly . . .

"Oh God," she whispered, "the Gold Special's on. Nudge it left, Sta-Hi."

He twitched some English onto the ball. It caromed off a pad angled just so, and snugged into the gold socket nestled between two big outs. The machine THHOCCKKKKED. And shut itself off.

Sta-Hi pushed his trigger. Nothing happened. "What . . ."

"We beat it!" Wendy squeaked. "We took it all the way! Let's go get the pay-off!"

"But I thought there was just . . ." Sta-Hi pulled open the drawer in the machine's front. A ticket for five free meals at McDonald's.

"Sure there's *that*," Wendy said. "But the cashier has to give me five hundred dollars, too. Special Daytona rules."

Sta-Hi followed Wendy to the cashier, and out onto the street. She wore green cut-off over-alls, and sandals with thongs criss-crossing up her legs. He had to hurry to keep up with her. It was like she was trying to lose him.

"Where are you going, Wendy? Slow down! Half that money's mine!" He caught her lightly by her bare brown arm.

"Let go!" She twitched her arm free. "That money isn't yours *or* mine. It's all for Personetics. Good-bye!" Without even looking at him, she strode on down the sidewalk.

"You whore!" Sta-Hi shouted angrily. "That's *it*, isn't it! You've got your night's money now and you'll give it to your greaser sex-pistol and catch some sleep!" He ran after her, and grabbed her arm, hard this time. "Give me my two-hundred-fifty bucks!"

Wendy burst into tears. Fake? "I'm not a p-prostitute. It's just f-flirty-fishing. Personetics needs the money for more hardware. To save everyone's soul."

Hardware? Souls? A contact at last.

"You can keep the money," Sta-Hi said, not loosening his grip. "But I want to come back with you. I want to join Personetics."

She looked into his eyes, trying to read his intentions. "Do you really? Do you want to be saved? Personetics isn't just another cult, you know. It's for real."

Sta-Hi examined her closely, trying to decide if . . . Finally he popped the question.

"Are you a robot?"

"No." Wendy shook her head. "I'm not really saved yet. But Mel is. Mel Nast. He's our leader. Do you want to meet him?"

"I sure do. I'm a bopper-lover from way back. How far is it to the temple?"

"Forty kays. We're in the old Marineland building."

"Are we supposed to walk or what?"

"Usually I wait till five AM. That's when Mr. Nast comes and picks us all up. The boys sell things, and the girls go flirty-fishing all night long. But if you get your five hundred dollars early you can go back to Mel. Do you have a car or a bike?"

Sta-Hi's hydrogen motorcycle was long gone. He hadn't seen it since that Friday he'd left it chained up in front of the Lido Hotel. After that he'd met Misty, and the Little Kidders . . . and then it had been Cocoa and the Moon and all that. How long had it been, two months? It felt like finally things were going to happen again.

"I'll get a car," Sta-Hi said. "I'll steal a car."

"That would be nice," Wendy said. "Mel would like you if you brought him a car."

But how? In Daytona, nobody was fool enough to leave his key in the ignition. Suddenly Sta-Hi thought of a way. He'd get his taxi back.

"Go wait for me by McDonald's, Wendy. I'll be back with a car in half an hour."

The Yellow Cab terminal was only five blocks off. Malley, the dispatcher, was sitting in a glass booth at the garage entrance, same as ever. Looking past him, Sta-Hi saw that Number Eleven, his old cab, was idle tonight.

"Hey, Malley, you lame son of death, stop jerking off and gimme my keys." Best defense is a good offense.

Malley glared, nothing moving but his tiny eyes. "Bullshit, Mooney. You can't just quit and walk back on the job any time you like. You're too stoned to drive anyway. Giddaddahere."

"Come on, Pappy Dear-smear, I need the dust, you must? I'm eating sand out there. Put me on and I'll kick you ten percent."

"Twenty," Malley said, holding up the keys. "And if you fuck up again you're out for good. I don't live to keep you in dope."

Sta-Hi took the keys. "You can *die* to keep me in dope for all I care. Live or die, just keep me high."

After ten days off, it felt nice to be back in Lucky Eleven. They must not have found a new driver for it, since the cab still had all of Sta-Hi's personal touches. There was the fake come-spot on the roof over his head, the skull with the red-lite eyes in the back window, the plastic fur rug on the floor . . . and even the tape-deck was still there. How could he have walked off the job and forgotten his tape-deck!

He had the cab wired for sound, so he could record his monologues, or interview the passengers. The cab started up right away, and then he was out on the street, thinking about his tape-recorder. It made a big impression on chicks, made them think he was an agent. Funny word: *agent*.

A gent. Age entity. Ageing tea. Aegean Sea. A.G.C. Now what did that *A.G.C.* stand for?

If he hadn't seen Wendy standing in front of McDonald's just then, Sta-Hi probably would have forgot-

ten all about her. Being back in the cab had zapped him
into a conditioned reflex of head-tripping and driving the
strip. But there was Wendy, bright and blonde in her
tight cut-offs. Foxy fish.

He pulled over and she got in back.

"Number Eleven," Malley was saying, "there's a call
at Km. 13."

"I just got a fare, Malley. Two gentlemen want to go
to Cocoa."

"That'll be an out of zone charge," Malley re-
sponded. "Check in when you get back. That *was* twenty
percent."

"Over dover." He turned the squawker off.

"How did you get the cab?" Wendy asked, wide-
eyed. "Did you hurt the driver?"

"Not at all," Sta-Hi said, pointing to the dark stain
over his head. "See the come-spot?"

"I don't understand."

"I'm a cab-driver. This is my cab. If I like it at Marineland I'll give Personetics the cab and stay there. Oth-
erwise I'll go back to work, and I'll just have to pay that
fare to Cocoa myself. Come up in front and sit next to
me."

She climbed over the seat. They split a jay, driving
slow with the windows down. It was nice to be driving
again. It felt like the car was on rails, a toy train tootling
through the palmy night.

Chapter Twenty-six

The old Marineland had closed down back in 2007, after a hurricane had caved in half the building. Now everyone who wanted to see the ritual degradation of dolphins had to go to Sea World instead. The building, in the middle of nowhere on Coastal Route 1A, came up on Sta-Hi unexpectedly.

"Pull around to the ocean side," Wendy said. "So no one sees."

"Yes ma'am. That'll be two fucks and a blow-job."

"Please, Sta-Hi, be serious. Not just anyone can become a member of Personetics. You have to have the right attitude."

"I'll try to keep it limp, baby."

There was a little parking lot in back. Sta-Hi pulled in next to a nice-looking red sedan. Off at the edge of the lot was a beat-up black truck. The wind was high, and the surf was loud. They got out and walked along a concrete wall to where a rusty door hung open. There were no lights inside.

"Mel," Wendy called at the top of her lungs. "I'm back already. I brought someone with another car for you."

There was the sound of footsteps, and a lithe figure hurried out of the building. He was the same height as Sta-Hi, and with the same rangy build. But his head . . . his big, round head seemed a size too big for the body. He made you think of a balloon tied to the end of a rope.

"Mel Nast," he said, sticking out his hand. He had a deep, sincere-sounding voice, with a trace of an East European accent. "I'm bleased to meet you. Vhat's your name?"

"I'm nobody," Sta-Hi said. "I'm Mr. Nobody from Nowhere."

"Don't listen to him, Mel. He told me his name is Sta-Hi. He says he's a bopper-lover from way back."

Spoken in Wendy's earnest treble the self description sounded pathetic, imbecilic. But Mel Nast looked sympathetic.

"The point is not just to love, Sta-Hi. It is to live. If only you can vake up in time. Blease come in."

Mel Nast's round head turned like a rotating planet, and his slender body followed along. The three of them walked down a damp corridor, through two doors and into a bright, windowless space.

It was a square hall, with big rectangular holes in the walls. One of the old tank-rooms. The aquarium glass had been smashed out and removed, and each of the tanks was now a sort of nook or roomlet. They followed Nast across the square floor and stopped before one of the ex-tanks. "STURGEON," a cracked label on the wall read, "*Acipenser Sturio.*"

There were two easy chairs in there, a shelf of books, and a desk covered with papers. "My study," the slim man with the big head explained. "Could you blease leave us now, Vhendy? I have plans to make with . . . Mister Hi." He flashed Sta-Hi a sudden smile. Had he *winked?*

"That's fine with me," Wendy said. "I'm all tired out. And here's tonight's take." She handed over the five-hundred-dollar bill and walked across the room. Apparently she had a bed in one of the tanks. Sta-Hi followed Nast into his study-tank. They sat down, and looked at each other in silence for a minute.

"How do you like my face?" Nast asked finally. The round face was dominated by a fleshy nose, from which two wrinkles ran down, suspending the somewhat sensual mouth in a rounded sling of folds. The lips parted, revealing square, uniform teeth. "Should I change it?"

"It depends on what you want to do," Sta-Hi said uncertainly.

"What do *you* want to do?" came the answer. "What do you want from the boppers?"

Another hard question. Most superficially, Sta-Hi wanted to acquire another Happy Cloak and use it to get famous. But on another level, hardly conscious, he wanted revenge, revenge for his father's death, revenge for what the nursie had done to Cobb Anderson.

He hated the boppers. But he loved them. The diggers . . . the diggers had helped him. Wearing the Happy Cloak and raiding the factory had been fantastic. Perhaps what he really wanted was to go back to Disky and help in the civil war, loving and hating at the same time.

Something strange happened to Mel Nast's face while Sta-Hi considered his answer. The fatty puffed-out skin tightened, the cheeks drew in, and a white beard blossomed around the mouth. Suddenly he was looking at . . .

"Cobb?" Sta-Hi asked. "Is it you?" He started to smile and then stopped. "You killed my father! You . . ."

"I *had* to, Sta-Hi. You heard him. He said he was going to have me dismantled!"

"So? It wouldn't have killed you. You blew up your body along with his, and now you're still here and he's gone forever!" The grief came welling up at last, and Sta-Hi's voice quavered.

"He wasn't such a bad guy. And he could paint spaceships better than anyone I ever . . ." Sta-Hi broke off, sobbing. A minute went by till he found his voice again.

"I saw them take you apart, Cobb. They took out your heart and your balls and everything else. It's like . . ." The face across from him looked sympathetic, interested. The perfect cult minister.

"Fuck!" Sta-Hi spat, suddenly lashing out and hitting the robot's face with the back of his hand. "I might as well be talking to a tape-recorder."

The blow hurt his hand, and made him angrier. He got to his feet, standing over the Cobb-faced robot.

"I ought to fucking take you apart!"

The robot began to talk then, slowly, and in Cobb's old voice. "Listen to me, Sta-Hi. Sit down and listen. You know perfectly well that you can't hurt me by hammering on this robot-remote. I'm sorry your father died. But death isn't real. You have to understand that. Death is meaningless. I wasted the last ten years being scared of death, and now . . ."

"Now that you think you're immortal you don't worry about death," Sta-Hi said bitterly. "That's really enlightened of you. But whether you know it or not, Cobb Anderson is *dead*. I saw him die, and if you think you're him, you're just fooling yourself." He sat down, suddenly very tired.

"If I'm not Cobb Anderson, then who would I be?" The flicker-cladding face smiled at him gently. "I *know* I'm Cobb. I have the same memories, the same habits, the same feelings that I always did."

"But what about your . . . your *soul*," Sta-Hi said, not liking to use the word. "Each person has a soul, a consciousness, whatever you call it. There's some special thing that makes a person be alive, and there's no way that can go into a computer program. No way."

"*It* doesn't have to go into the program, Sta-Hi. *It* is everywhere. *It* is just existence itself. All consciousness is One. The One is God. God is pure existence unmodified."

Cobb's voice was intense, evangelical. "A person is just hardware plus software plus existence. Me existing in flesh is the same as me existing on chips. But that's not all.

"*Potential* existence is as good as *actual* existence. That's why death is impossible. Your software exists permanently and indestructably as a certain *possibility*, a certain mathematical set of relations. Your father is now an abstract, non-physical possibility. But nevertheless he exists! He . . ."

"What is this," Sta-Hi interrupted. "A cram-course in Personetics? Is this the crap that you feed those girls to keep them whoring for you? Forget it!"

Sta-Hi stopped talking, suddenly realizing something. That black truck outside . . . that must be the Mr. Frostee truck with a paint-job. And inside the truck would be a super-cooled big bopper brain with Cobb coded up inside it. He couldn't hurt this robot-remote, but if he got out to the truck . . . It was just a question of whether he really wanted to. Did he hate the boppers or not?

"I sense your hostility," Cobb said. "I respect that. But I'd like you to come in with me anyhow. I need an outside man, a Personetics promoter. I could be Jesus and you be John the Baptist. Or *you* be Jesus and I'll be God."

While he was talking, the robot's face changed again, to a copy of Sta-Hi's. "I always use this trick on the recruits," he chuckled. "Like Charlie Manson. *I am a mirror.* But that was before your time. Here, have a joint."

The robot lit a reefer and handed it over. The Cobb face came back. "I'm a little psychic now, too," he said. "I've gotten pretty loose. And what I said is really true. Nothing is ever really destroyed. There is no . . ."

"Oh, tape it," Sta-Hi said taking the reefer and leaning back in his easy chair. "I might come in with you. Especially if you can get me another Happy Cloak."

"What's that?" Cobb asked.

"Well, I never told you yet . . . about what I did on the Moon."

"You ran away in the museum. The next time I saw you, it was that night when you and your father . . ."

"Yeah, yeah," Sta-Hi said, cutting him off. "Don't remind me about that. Let me tell my story. I found this sort of cape called a Happy Cloak. It was made of flicker-cladding and when I put it on I could talk bopper, except with a Japanese accent. I went to where a bunch of boppers were storming a big factory called GAX. We got in, but GAX almost won anyway. Then at the last minute I blew him up."

The robot started in shock. "You blew up a big bopper?"

"Yeah. Some diggers and a repair spider had set the charge. All I had to do was push the button. The re-

motes would have gotten me then, but at the last minute
a digger tunneled up through the floor and saved me. He
took me to watch the nursie take you apart. Ralph and
the nursie taped you, and then the nursie grabbed Ralph
Numbers and taped him, too. The diggers said . . .''

Cobb's face was working, as if he were arguing with
a voice in his head. Now he interrupted. ''Mr. Frostee
wants to kill you, Sta-Hi. He says that if it weren't for
you blowing up GAX, the big boppers would have
won.''

Cobb was twitching now, as if he could hardly control
himself. His voice grew thin and odd. ''I'm not a puppet. Sta-Hi is my friend. I have free will.''

The words seemed to cost him a great effort. His eyes
kept straying to a hunting-knife lying on his desk.

''No!'' Cobb said, shaking his head jerkily. It wasn't
clear who he was talking to. ''I'm not your hand. I'm
your conscience! I'm a . . .''

Suddenly his voice stopped. The features of his face
clenched in a final spasm and then slid back into the se-
rene curves of Mel Nast. The thick lips parted to complete Cobb's sentence.

''. . . hallucination. But this robot-remote is, in the
last analysis, mine. I have temporarily had to evict Dr.
Anderson.'' The hand snaked over to pick up the knife.

Sta-Hi jumped to his feet and vaulted out of the tank
in one motion. He hit the floor running, with the robot
close behind.

The door out to the hall was open, and Sta-Hi managed to slam it behind him, gaining a few seconds. He
got the second door closed too, closed tight, and he had
his cab started by the time the robot came charging out.

Sta-Hi ignored it, and aimed his cab at the black panel
truck parked across the lot. He revved the engine up to
a chattering scream and peeled out.

The robot jumped onto his hood and punched his fist
through the windshield. Sta-Hi squinted against the flying
glass and kept the car aimed at the truck. He had it up
to fifty kph by the time it hit.

The air-bag in the steering column burst out, punching
Sta-Hi in the face and chest, keeping him in his seat. An

instant later the bag was limp and the car was stopped. Sta-Hi's lip had split. There was blood in his mouth. The car lights were out, and it was hard to see what had happened.

Footsteps came running across the parking lot.

"What happened? Sta-Hi? Mel?" It was Wendy. Sta-Hi got out of his cab. The girl ran past him, to reach out to the figure crushed between the cab and the dented side of the black van.

"Back up, Sta-Hi! Quick!"

But now the black van was moving instead. Its engine, already on, roared louder, and it backed out, grinding the pinned robot-remote against the cab's hood. It looked like steam was leaking from a hole in the truck's side.

The driverless van flicked its lights on, and Sta-Hi could make out the face of the broken robot slumped across his cab's hood. The blank eyes may have seen him or not, but then the lips moved. It was saying . . .

"Look out!" Sta-Hi screamed, snatching Wendy back and flinging their bodies to shelter on the ground behind the cab.

The robot-remote exploded, just like the other one had, back in the cottage on Cocoa Beach.

As the ringing of the explosion died out in their ears, they could hear the black van's engine, roaring south on Route One.

Chapter Twenty-seven

As soon as Mr. Frostee seized control of the remote, Cobb was utterly shut off from the outside world. As during his first transition, he felt a growing disorientation, an increasing blurring of all distinctions. But this time it stopped before getting completely out of control. Vision returned, and with it the ghosts of hands and feet. He was driving the truck.

"I'm sorry to have done that, Cobb. I was angry. It seemed essential to me to disassemble that young man as soon as possible."

"What's happened?" Cobb cried voicelessly. There was something funny about his vision. It was as if he were perched on top of the truck, instead of being behind the wheel. But yet he could *feel* the wheel, twitching back and forth as he steered the truck south. "What's happened?" he asked again.

"I just blew up my last remote. We're going to have to find someone to front for us. One of the Personetics people in Daytona."

"*Your* remote? That was supposed to be my body! I thought you said I had free will!"

"You still do. I can't make you change your mind about anything. But that body was mine as much as yours."

"Then how can I see? How can I drive?"

"The truck itself is a sort of body. There's two camera eyes that I can stick out of the roof. You're seeing through them. And I've turned the servos for manipulating the truck's controls over to you as well. We may have our occasional differences, Cobb, but I still trust you. Anyway, you're a better driver than I."

"I can't believe this," Cobb wailed. "Don't you have any survival instinct at all? I could have talked Sta-Hi into working with us!"

"He was the one who blew up GAX," Mr. Frostee replied. "And now the war is lost. BEX told me about it on the broadcast last week. Disky has reverted to complete anarchy. They've smashed most of MEX, and there's talk of disassembling TEX and even BEX as well. The final union is still . . . inevitable. But for now it looks as if . . ."

"As if what?" Cobb asked. There was a resigned and fatalistic edge to Mr. Frostee's words which terrified him.

"It's like waves, Cobb. Waves on the beach. Sometimes a wave comes up very far, past the tideline. A wave like that can carve out a new channel. The big boppers were a new channel. A higher form of life. But now we're sliding back . . . back into the sea, the sea of possibility. It doesn't matter. It's right, what you told the kids. Possible existence is as good as real existence."

They were driving into Daytona now. Lights flashed by. One of Cobb's "eyes" watched the road, and the other scanned the sidewalk, looking for one of the Personetics followers. The girls whored and the boys dealt dope. But it was so hard to remember their faces!

"You know," Mr. Frostee said. "You know he split the panels?"

"What do you mean?" There was nothing but darkness, and the two spots of vision, and the controls of the truck.

"There's heat leaking in from where your friend rammed us. The temperature's up five degrees. One more, and our circuits melt down. Thirty seconds, maybe."

"Am I on tape somewhere else?" Cobb asked. "Is there a copy on the Moon?"

"I don't know," Mr. Frostee said. "What's the difference?"

Chapter Twenty-eight

Wendy got the keys for the red sedan, and Sta-Hi drove them back to Daytona. They didn't talk much, but it was not a strained silence.

The police were all around the truck when they found it. Driverless, it had veered off the road, snapped a fire-hydrant, and smashed in the front of a Red Ball liquor-store. The police were worried about looting, and at first they wouldn't let Sta-Hi and Wendy through the line.

"That's my father!" Wendy screamed. "That's my father's truck!"

"She's right!" Sta-Hi added. "Let my poor wife through!"

"He's not in the truck now," a cop said, letting them approach. "Hey chief," he called then, "here's two in-dividuals who say they knew the driver."

The chief walked over, none other than Action Jackson. He had a mind like an FBI file, and recognized Sta-Hi instantly. "Young Mooney! Maybe you could en-laahten me as to what the *hail* is goin on?"

The crash had widened the rip in the truck's side, and clouds of helium were billowing out. The gas itself was invisible, but the low temperature filled the air with a mist of ice-crystals. A by-product of breathing the helium-rich air was that everyone's voice was coming out a bit high-pitched.

"There's a giant robot brain in the back," Sta-Hi piped. "A big bopper. It's the same one that killed my father and tried to eat my brain."

Jackson looked doubtful. "A truck tried to eat your brain?" He raised his voice, "Hey, Don! You and Steve open tup! See whut's in back!"

"Be careful!" Wendy squeaked, but by then the door was open. When the mist dispersed you could see Don and Steve reaching in and poking around with billy-clubs. There was a sound of breaking glass.

"Whooo-ee!" Don called. "Got nuff goodies in here to open us a Radio Shack! Steve and me saw it first!" He swirled his club around, and there was more tinkling from inside the truck.

The others walked over to look in. The truck was lying half keeled-over. There was a lot of frost inside, like in a freezer chest. The liquid-helium vessel that had surrounded Mr. Frostee was broken and there in the center was a big, intricate lump of chips and wires.

"Who was drivin?" Action Jackson wanted to know.

"It could drive itself," Sta-Hi said. "I rammed it and made a hole. It must have heated up too much."

"You a hero, boy," Jackson said admiringly. "You may amount to something yet."

"If I'm a hero, can I leave now?"

A hard glance, and then a nod. "Awright. You come in tomorrow make a deposition and I might could get you a reward."

Sta-Hi helped himself to a bottle from the liquor-store window and went back to the car with Wendy. He let her drive. She pulled down a ramp onto the beach, and they parked on the hard sand. He got the bottle open: white wine.

"Here," Sta-Hi said, passing her the wine. "And why did you say he was your father?"

"Why did you say I was your wife?"

"Why not?"

The moon scudded in and out of clouds, and the waves came in long smooth tubes.